W.i.t.c.h.

Will   Irma   Taranee   Cornelia   Hay Lin

Illusions and Lies

Adapted by ELIZABETH LENHARD

VOLO
an imprint of
HYPERION BOOKS FOR CHILDREN
New York

© 2004 Disney Enterprises, Inc.

W.I.T.C.H. Will Irma Taranee Cornelia Hay Lin is a trademark of Disney Enterprises, Inc.
Volo® is a registered trademark of Disney Enterprises, Inc.
Volo/Hyperion Books for Children are imprints of Disney Children's Group, L.L.C.

Printed in the United States of America

3 5 7 9 10 8 6 4 2

This book is set in 12/16.5 Hiroshige Book.
ISBN 0-7868-1795-X
Visit www.clubwitch.com

ON EARTH, SOME TIME LATER, IN THE HEATHERFIELD SPORTS CENTER . . .

COME ON, WILL! TWO MORE STROKES.

YEEESSS!

FRUUUSH

GREAT TIME! GOOD JOB, WILL!

THANKS, VERA! BUT WITHOUT YOUR HELP, I WOULD NEVER HAVE DONE IT,

EVER SINCE YOU STARTED TRAINING ME, I'VE BEEN IN GREAT SHAPE. DO YOU REALLY HAVE TO GO AWAY?

I'M ONLY FILLING IN FOR THE HEAD TRAINER, WHO IS COMING BACK SOON. BUT LET'S FOCUS ON YOU RIGHT NOW, OKAY?

I SIGNED YOU UP FOR THE SCHOOL CHAMPIONSHIPS THAT ARE TAKING PLACE HERE.

ARE YOU SERIOUS?

OF COURSE I'M SERIOUS. I ALREADY MENTIONED YOUR NAME TO THE DIRECTORS OF THE SHEFFIELD INSTITUTE.

THAT'S FANTASTIC!

IF YOU ARE CHOSEN, YOU WILL HAVE TO TRAIN EVERY DAY. I NEED TO GET YOUR MOTHER'S PERMISSION.

NO PROBLEM! I'LL TALK TO HER ABOUT IT TONIGHT, AT DINNER.

WOW! I CAN'T BELIEVE I WAS ABLE TO ACHIEVE MY GOAL, WITHOUT USING MY POWERS.

FINALLY, I CAN SHOW THEM HOW GOOD I AM. MOM WILL BE ENTHUSIASTIC ABOUT IT!

BUT, ON THE CONTRARY . . .

MY ANSWER IS NO!

WHAT?

YOU HEARD ME! NOW, HELP ME CLEAR THE TABLE.

I STILL DON'T UNDERSTAND! WHY?

YOU CAN'T WASTE TIME TRAINING! YOU HAVE TO STUDY. YOUR GRADES ARE TOO LOW.

WHO TOLD YOU THAT? IT WAS COLLINS, WASN'T IT? THAT . . .

WATCH WHAT YOU SAY! YOUR HISTORY TEACHER IS ALSO MY GOOD FRIEND.

HE NOT ONLY MORTIFIED ME IN FRONT OF MY FRIENDS, BUT NOW HE IS SPYING ON ME!

STOP IT!

I COULD HAVE RAISED MY GRADE BEFORE THE COMPETITION, BUT YOU'VE ALREADY DRAWN YOUR CONCLUSIONS.

SLAM

THE NEXT MORNING, IN FRONT OF THE SHEFFIELD INSTITUTE...

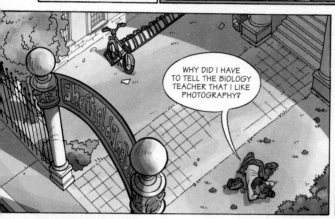

WHY? WHY?

WHY DID I HAVE TO TELL THE BIOLOGY TEACHER THAT I LIKE PHOTOGRAPHY?

"THAT'S WONDERFUL, TARANEE! TAKE A PHOTO OF THREE BUGS AND MAKE A CONNECTION, DARLING!"

THERE'S JUST ONE PROBLEM: BUGS DISGUST ME!

AND THEY LOOK EVEN BIGGER WITH A ZOOM LENS!

A BUTTERFLY! MY SAVIOR!

STOP JUST A MINUTE, BEAUTIFUL BUTTERFLY. STOP! STOP A LITTLE, DON'T MOVE YOUR LITTLE WINGS. . . .

FRUSH

ONE

Taranee Cook groaned as she crept across the lawn on her hands and knees. She just *knew* she was getting grass stains on her favorite purple jeans. What's more, her round glasses kept slipping down her nose, and the beaded ends of her long braids trailed in the dirt.

I would give anything to abandon this mission, Taranee thought with a sigh. If only I could!

And what is my mission? Taranee thought, flicking a ticklish blade of grass away from her nose. Conjuring up a fireball in the palm of my hand, perhaps, to toss at some slimy, blue monster? Or using my magic to close a gateway between earth and a faraway, evil universe? Maybe I have to escape the clutches of Elyon,

a girl who used to be my friend, but is now this otherworldly princess of darkness.

Or maybe, Taranee thought with a rueful laugh, I simply have to save the world.

It could have been any of the above. Not too long ago, Taranee had been transformed from an ordinary girl—your average shutterbug and shy new student at the Sheffield Institute—into a Guardian of the Veil.

This Veil was not bridal nor made of lace. This Veil was made of bigger stuff. In fact, it covered the entire world! It was a cosmic barrier that separated earth—otherwise known as home of the good guys—from Metamoor, an unknown, primitive land populated by reptilian creatures. Many of the creatures looked like massive lizards, albeit ones who dressed in suede tunics. Others were blue giants with craggy, rocklike horns upon their heads. Still others had red eyes, dreadlocks, and stolid bodies clad in rhinoesque armor.

It's like a bad horror movie, right? Taranee asked herself with an incredulous, dry laugh.

Not really. Many of those creatures were as kind and caring as any human. They cooked meals, raised their kids, and built thatched-roof homes, like any other old-fashioned townspeople. The only difference between them and the residents of Heatherfield—the hip, seaside city where Taranee lived—was in their form of government.

Make that *dictatorship*.

A cloud of oppression kept Metamoor in gloomy shadows. The person responsible for that state of affairs was a brutal prince named Phobos—a young man so vain only a select few were allowed to gaze upon his face.

With nobody to rein his evil self in, Phobos used Metamoor for his own pleasure. He hoarded all the planet's natural resources to create an Eden for himself. He left his people to toil in hardscrabble villages. He stole not only their sunshine but their hope.

And was that enough? Not even. Phobos and his evil minions also wanted a piece of earth.

Boy, Taranee thought as she shifted her position on the grass. If I thought Metamoor was hard to conceive of, Candracar is positively preposterous.

Candracar existed "in the middle of infinity." Taranee's image of it was filled with clouds, looming temples, and beatific specters in gossamer cloaks. But that was all speculation. Taranee had never been to Candracar. It was as fantastic to her as fairyland.

The Veil was proof that hope existed. Someone in Candracar had created the Veil. And for centuries, it had kept Metamoorians away from earth, and vice versa. Nobody could stop the dawning of the millennium. When the year 2000 struck, the Veil had weakened. Twelve fissures had opened in the barrier. Eventually, those cracks had become portals, which were sort of cosmic superhighways between earth and Metamoor.

Taranee shuddered at the thought of those strange tunnels running from one galaxy to the next. She had traveled through a couple of portals and, each time, it had been an exceedingly rough ride!

The problem was, Taranee wasn't the only one traveling by portal. Some of Phobos's followers had been using them, too—to try to invade earth.

That was why Taranee had been anointed with magical powers. She had been given the role of fire starter, able to whip up flames, redirect a rocket, or quell a forest fire, all with little more than mere determination.

Taranee's best friends had been brought on board, too. Irma was all about water, and Hay Lin was all things air. Cornelia controlled the earth, and Will was their leader, the keeper of the glowy orb called the Heart of Candracar. Whenever she unleashed the glass pendant's powers, the girls were transformed into beautiful, knowing, young women—complete with mod, winged, purple-and-turquoise outfits. Their club even had a cool title: the names Will, Irma, Taranee, Cornelia, and Hay Lin, spelled W.i.t.c.h.

Some parts of being a Guardian, Taranee had to admit, were fun.

I mean, she thought with a shrug, at first I was freaked about being, well, magical. But soon, I realized conjuring fire was kinda . . . cool!

Of course, with magic powers came magic responsibilities—daunting ones, at that.

Their job as members of W.i.t.c.h. was to close every portal that had erupted between earth and Metamoor. And with monsters constantly breaking through those openings, the task wasn't always that easy!

To add insult to injury, the girls' former friend, Elyon, had been swayed into defecting to Metamoor. A cute-boy-turned-snaky-Metamoorian named Cedric had told Elyon she was Phobos's sister. According to Cedric's story, the infant Elyon had been snatched away from Metamoor to be raised as a humble human child on earth. Elyon had been filled with rage when she discovered how many years of royal treatment had been denied her. She'd tried to get her friends to cross over to Metamoor's dark side with her, and, when they had refused, she had become their enemy. In fact, it seemed she was there, to sabotage their mission every time the Guardians turned around.

Just the thought of it made Taranee's narrow shoulders sag with weariness. But as she inched farther along on the lawn, she realized that, at that moment at least, she had nothing to worry about.

There's no way, she thought with a shrug, that Elyon would care at all about my current mission.

Because, at the moment, Taranee *wasn't* closing a portal or saving the world.

No, she was crawling across the grass in

front of her school doing a homework assignment—and an especially gross one at that!

"Why, why, why," she muttered, "did I have to go and tell my biology teacher that I love photography?"

She lapsed into the breathy, nasal voice of her teacher. "'Good, Taranee,'" she mimicked. "'Take pictures of three bugs and write a report, dear.'"

"Ugh," Taranee shuddered, speaking now in her own voice—which was throaty and always on the quiet side. "There's only one little problem with this assignment. Bugs totally skeeve me out!"

Clenching her teeth in disgust, Taranee uncapped her camera lens and lifted the camera to her bespectacled eye. She slowly scanned the lawn. The blades of grass were as big as elephant ears by now. And, sure enough, nestled among them, she discovered a grotesque beetle. Its antennae quivered and danced in the brisk morning breeze.

"Ewww!" Taranee squealed, lowering the camera quickly. "I think it's time to ditch the zoom lens!" Bugs weren't meant to be big.

She unscrewed the lens—a fabulous gadget

that her dad had given her for her last birthday. The gift had been a no-brainer for her psychologist dad. He was all about self-expression, and he jumped at every opportunity to draw Taranee out of her shell, especially since the Cook family had moved to Heatherfield only recently. His thinking: what's a better ice-breaker than shooting a close-up of someone?

The thought made Taranee smile. She should tell her dad she'd been doing just fine in the friendship department, even without her camera. She and Will had become soul mates even before they found out they were destined to save the world together. And she felt a real connection with the other Guardians, too. That part surprised her. Will was shy like her, but the other girls weren't, in the slightest.

After all, we're as different as, well, earth, water, wind, and fire, Taranee thought, with a little giggle. Irma's this bouncy flirt who's more at home at the mall than in any math class. Cornelia's tall, elegant, and completely poised. Meanwhile, Hay Lin's a tiny little thing who'd be bouncing off the walls even if she didn't have jet-puffs of air on her side.

But somehow, Taranee mused, we all seem to fit together. We're a team.

Now, she thought, as she fitted a less . . . bug-eyed lens onto her camera, if only I could get my friends to help me with this assignment!

Curling her lip in disgust, Taranee gazed through the viewfinder again. And once again, she gasped. But this time, it wasn't in disgust! She'd somehow homed right in on the only *non*gross bug nature had to offer—a butterfly! It was perched on a blade of grass, its iridescent blue wings fluttering lazily.

"My savior!" Taranee whispered with a grin. She inched forward on her elbows to get a better angle.

"Stop just a minute, pretty little thing," Taranee murmured as she twisted her lens for a better focus. She almost had the perfect shot!

"Stop," Taranee crooned again to the delicate insect. "Don't move your wings and . . ."

Taranee's finger was just closing on the shutter when suddenly, the butterfly flitted away in fright! In its place, a big, dirty, red object landed in the grass with a rude *whomp*.

Through her camera, Taranee now found herself staring at a very floppy, and very stinky, red high top. It was the kind of decrepit sneaker that could only belong to . . . a boy.

Taranee scowled and looked up. First she saw a saggy, dark sock. Then a pair of knobby knees and some baggy, brown shorts. Finally, she found herself gazing at the thin-lipped sneer of . . .

"Uriah!" Taranee cried.

Ugh, she thought. If it's not blue monsters popping out of portals, it's that needle-nosed Uriah.

Uriah was the king of the Outfielders—the burnouts and brutes that lurked on the fringes of the Sheffield Institute's social order. They were bullies who found every opportunity to dis the popular kids and the science geeks alike.

Uriah was an Outfielder extraordinaire—the equal-opportunity abuser type. He tortured Infielders, jocks, small animals . . . even his own loyal gang members! Taranee had spied on Uriah and seen him leading his gang around like a prison guard. The big brute Laurent, with his buzz-cut hair, and potbellied Kurt seemed only too happy to be Uriah's yes-men. It was pathetic.

But Nigel, the fourth member of Uriah's gang, seemed different. He didn't sport anything like Uriah's greasy zits or Kurt and Laurent's dopey attitudes. In fact, the last time Taranee had peeked at Nigel, he'd looked practically perfect. His silky, brown hair fell in casual waves to his chin, which was strong and scruffiness-free.

What really got to Taranee were Nigel's brown eyes. They were as soft and sad as an abandoned puppy's.

And with good reason, Taranee thought, as she glared up at Uriah. The whole gang had recently gotten into major trouble.

It had all started when Irma had gone to the Heatherfield Museum. As often happened when Irma hit the town, the gregarious girl ran into someone she knew. But this time it was no friendly acquaintance. It was a lizard from Metamoor! It turned out that the museum was home to a portal!

While the Guardians were busy dealing with the Veil's latest fissure, word had gotten out about the strange creature at the museum. Uriah had been as drawn to the rumor as a rat is to cheese. He'd goaded his gang into breaking into the museum in the middle of the night for a little monster hunt.

Naturally, the guys had been snagged by security. They'd been brought to the police station, where they'd faced Judge Theresa Cook—otherwise known as Taranee's mother!

Taranee's mom had ordered the gang to do a year of community service in the very museum they'd infiltrated. Soon afterward, Taranee had seen Nigel there, wearing the telltale orange jumpsuit of a kid doing time.

As Nigel had dusted sculptures and swept the museum floors, Taranee had caught his gaze from across a gallery full of paintings. She could still remember the sensation. All the beautiful artwork had melted from her peripheral vision. Nigel's ugly jumpsuit had faded into a blur, too. Taranee had seen only Nigel's brown eyes—eyes that were kind and pretty and . . . crinkled up in a shy smile. At her!

Now, here on Sheffield's front lawn, those eyes were focused on her again. Nigel had arrived on the scene with Kurt and Laurent, right after Uriah. But this time, Nigel wasn't smiling.

When Uriah shoved his oily face into Taranee's—totally blocking her view of cute Nigel—she realized why her crush looked so stricken. Uriah hadn't just stumbled upon Taranee. No—she was his target!

"Look who's here," Uriah growled. "The judge's daughter."

Normally, that would have been the moment when Taranee melted into a puddle. Confrontation had never been her bag. What could she say? Battling the forces of evil with immense stores of her own magic had boosted her confidence.

So instead of caving, she merely glared at Uriah and demanded, "What do you want?"

"Only to tell you that, thanks to your mother, we'll be spending the next year in that stupid museum," Uriah snarled. "Cleaning galleries, dusting artwork, and doing other ridiculous chores."

While Taranee responded with a scornful smirk, Nigel stepped forward and placed a placating hand on Uriah's arm.

"C'mon, dude," he said, haltingly. "Kids are starting to show up."

"Shut up, Nigel," Uriah spat, without releasing Taranee from his glare. When she glared back, unintimidated, Uriah reached out and cupped her chin in his rough fingers. Taranee held her breath.

"I only want this little girl to understand who she's dealing with," Uriah continued. "After all, her family has just arrived in town. She might not get—"

"There are tons of people on the stairs!" Nigel said with alarm.

The next thing Taranee knew, a familiar voice had invaded the space.

"Wassup, Taranee?"

Uriah jumped. His hands unclenched and fell to his sides. He replaced his threatening glare with a mere sneer. Then he turned around to see who had come to Taranee's rescue.

Imagine his surprise when the hero turned out to be a spindly Asian girl with long pigtails and goofy, purple goggles perched atop her head.

A girl, moreover, who was completely alone.

"Tons of people?" Uriah sputtered. He glared accusingly at Nigel. "I see *one* little girl, you idiot."

Nigel shot Taranee a furtive glance. Then he shrugged at Uriah and said sullenly, "From here, it looked like more."

Taranee felt a burst of warmth fill her chest. Nigel had totally rescued her! He'd spotted Hay Lin and spoken up loudly enough to attract her attention. Then he had lied to Uriah to protect her. He was so romantic!

He was also, clearly, one of the good guys. Taranee just knew it. The only mystery was—what was he doing hanging out with these creeps?

There was no time to ask him.

"C'mon, boys," Uriah ordered his crew. "We'll continue this conversation another time."

The group shuffled off.

As Taranee gazed after them—well, after Nigel—she felt a small hand alight upon her shoulder.

"Everything all right, Taranee?" Hay Lin asked her. Her eyes, usually dancing with fun, were dark with concern. "Were they bothering you?"

"It's all right, now," Taranee said with a grateful smile. It seemed that whenever she got into a bind these days—whether she was late to history class or kidnapped and imprisoned in dark Metamoor—her fellow Guardians popped up at her side. Taranee felt as though she could count on them for anything.

Well . . . *almost* anything.

"Those guys were just blowing off steam," Taranee said, turning from Hay Lin to watch the gang stomp away. Nigel was trailing behind them. In fact, he was stopping altogether. Taranee watched him take a deep breath, then brush a shock of glossy hair out of his eyes as he turned to peek backward.

He was looking for Taranee!

Once again, she caught the boy's shy gaze.

With her heart in her throat, Taranee wondered what to do. She knew what the *old* Taranee would have done. She'd have ducked behind the safety of her camera. Or quickly darted beneath a tree to stick her nose in a book. She would have flown away just like one of the skittish insects darting around the lawn.

But now, things were different. She had fire in the palm of her hand. And she had her friend, Hay Lin, at her side.

So . . . Taranee shot Nigel a smile—not a big one, mind you—but broad enough to show, she hoped, that she was smitten.

Nigel returned her smile. Then he waved at her! Finally, regretfully, he turned to continue plodding after his crew.

Taranee closed her eyes for a moment. She felt as though she'd just swallowed a spoonful of honey, followed by a shot of espresso! Who knew you could feel so gooey and so hyped at the same time? Not to mention . . . wistful.

"Yeah," she sighed to Hay Lin, as Nigel headed off. "Everything's okay, except for one little problem. How will I find my butterfly again?"

TWO

Cornelia Hale folded her slender body in to her seat and pulled out her history book. When she'd opened the book to chapter seven and neatly pressed the pages into place, she looked around the classroom.

It was the usual A.M. scene. Sheffielders were dragging themselves into first-period class like prisoners showing up for assigned duty. Backpacks landed on the floor with dull thuds. Kids yawned widely. They popped breath mints into their mouths. And then they continued whatever gossip sessions they'd started on Sheffield's front lawn before the bell had rung.

Donny Lipsitz, always the last to arrive in class, took a final swig from his soda as he stumbled into the room. Then he crushed the can and sprawled in his seat.

The only thing missing, Cornelia noticed with raised eyebrows, was Will. Donny Lipsitz had beat Will to class—and that wasn't a good sign.

Well, Cornelia thought drily, it looks like I'm discovering yet another side of Will—the rebellious *and* late teenager.

Ever since she'd met Will, Cornelia had had a hard time pinning her down. Her other friends were easier to peg—Irma was the prankster, always trying to push Cornelia's buttons. Taranee was the shy voice of reason, and Hay Lin was the peacemaker, who could smooth ruffled feathers. She did it with a grin and perhaps a temporary tattoo she'd draw with a Magic Marker on her friend's hand.

But Will . . . she was a different story. At first, she'd seemed like a poster child for low self-esteem. New to Heatherfield, with her parents' divorce weighing heavily on her, she'd stumbled into the Sheffield Institute looking pale and frightened. She'd been one big, raw nerve.

She certainly hadn't seemed like leader

material. Yet the Oracle of Candracar had made her the leader of W.i.t.c.h.—the Keeper of the Heart. As reluctant as Cornelia had been to defer to her little redheaded friend, Will had been just as ambivalent about guiding the group.

But lately, Will's nervousness had begun to melt away. In fact, the Heart of Candracar that hovered inside her body seemed to have infused her with strength and wisdom. Will's power had helped the whole group to get out of several deadly predicaments.

Though dubious, Cornelia had had to hand it to Will—perhaps she had what it took to lead their little save-the-world club.

Maybe she does, Cornelia thought as she uncapped her favorite pen. And maybe she doesn't. After all, Will has a habit of letting her emotions get in the way of her mission. Especially when that mission is making it to history class on time!

Cornelia knew Will's no-show wasn't about oversleeping or disciplining her crazy pet dormouse. No, it was all about their history teacher, Mr. Collins, otherwise known as Will's mother's new boyfriend!

Cornelia couldn't imagine having parents who were divorced or moving to a new city, much less having her mom date her teacher. She and her parents had lived in the same penthouse apartment all her life. Even though Lilian, Cornelia's little sister, was something of a brat, she, too. was part of Cornelia's family.

Then, Cornelia had sprouted wings and started making trees grow out of the earth on a whim, or carving holes in stone walls with a flick of her fingers. She'd even traveled through otherworldly wormholes to savage and distant planets.

And Cornelia had thought *puberty* was awkward! To say that her oh-so-placid life had hit a rough spot when she'd gone magical would be the understatement of the century.

It must be even worse for Will, Cornelia realized. Imagine, having to see your mom's boyfriend in class every morning—major mortification moment!

As if to fuel Cornelia's sympathetic thoughts, Mr. Collins walked into the classroom, just as the tardy bell rang. Cornelia peered past her mild-mannered teacher. Will was nowhere in sight!

To make matters worse, Mr. Collins wasn't looking nearly as mild-mannered as he usually did. In fact, his honey-colored mustache was twitching viciously, and he had a cruel gleam in his eyes.

"Good morning, guys," Mr. Collins said, scanning the faces of the still-yawning students. As usual, the only acknowledgment any of the kids paid to their teacher's entrance was a downshift in their chattering. Instead of yelling across the aisles, they now huddled together and started whispering.

"Oh, get comfortable," Mr. Collins continued drily. "Don't get up on my behalf."

"Huh?" Donny Lipsitz grunted, looking around the classroom with lazy eyes. Then he slouched farther into his chair and planted his tattered black basketball shoes on his desk. "Who was getting up, Mr. Collins?"

"I was being sarcastic, Lipsitz," Mr. Collins spat. "Get your feet off your desk and tell me where Will Vandom is."

Cornelia felt a chill run through her. Will was in for it, now. Maybe she could try to run some type of interference.

"I know where she is!" Cornelia piped up.

She clicked and unclicked her pink pen-top nervously. "She . . . went to the bathroom. You weren't here for her to ask, so . . ."

"The fact that I'm late," Mr. Collins said, "doesn't justify her leaving without permission."

Mr. Collins sat at his desk and opened his textbook. His mustache twitched irritably again as he brusquely flipped through the book's pages. It looked as if he were suddenly unaccustomed to having that brushlike fuzz beneath his nose—even though Mr. Collins had had a mustache for as long as Cornelia could remember. It was his trademark.

Donny Lipsitz was completely oblivious, of course, to the fact that Mr. Collins was clearly in a *mood*.

"But, Mr. Collins," he said slowly. "If you're not here, who are we supposed to ask permission from?"

Mr. Collins didn't even glance up from his book. He merely jerked his thumb toward the classroom door.

"Principal Knickerbocker's office—now," he ordered Donny. "You know the way."

Heaving a huge sigh, Donny lurched out of

his chair and headed out the door, a confused look on his face.

You're in a bad mood today, aren't you? Donny mused when he got to the door. Okay, so we'll play that game.

With that, Donny ran a hand through his spiky brown hair and slumped through the door. The moment he disappeared out the door, another figure appeared—one with sullen, brown eyes and bony shoulders hunched up to the ends of her tousled, red bob.

Mr. Collins gave the girl a sarcastic smile.

"Will!" he announced with mock cheer. "Welcome back. It's a pleasure to see you."

Will cast her eyes downward and began to slump to her desk, next to Cornelia's. But as she passed Mr. Collins's desk, she stumbled. Her eyelids fluttered and she uttered a brief, soft moan.

Cornelia blinked in surprise. She knew Will was angsting about Mr. Collins and her mom, but going pale and faint was a bit dramatic, wasn't it?

Will quickly shook off her queasy feeling. She gave Mr. Collins a sidelong look, then made her way to her desk. She carefully lowered herself into her chair and wiped away a layer of sweat that had formed on her upper lip.

"What's wrong, Will?" Cornelia whispered, leaning over to gaze at her friend with concern.

"Nothing," Will said, but her voice was filled with uncertainty. She glanced at Mr. Collins again. He was still turning the pages of his book, his mustache twitching away.

"When I passed by him," Will whispered to Cornelia, "I felt dizzy."

Cornelia shrugged.

"Maybe you didn't get enough sleep last night," Cornelia said. "Or you're hungry."

"No," Will said, giving Mr. Collins another glance. This time, it was heavy with hostility and suspicion.

"It's the same feeling I have whenever I'm near a portal," she whispered. "Or a being from Metamoor."

Cornelia shook her head in confusion. She'd seen Will go limp, pale, and shaky in the presence of Metamoorian magic. It was almost as if the evil of Metamoor and the good of Candracar were duking it out in the girl's head! Cornelia might have envied Will's special role as the Heart of Candracar's keeper, but she definitely didn't covet those fainting spells. They looked awful.

But did they *always* mean that evil was lurking about? Cornelia glanced at Mr. Collins skeptically. The worst thing he seemed capable of was assigning too much homework. The truth was, the Guardians had barely had their powers long enough for them to recognize any patterns in all this magical madness.

Before Cornelia could muse any further about Will's dizzy spell, a more pressing issue emerged.

"This year's program is extensive," Mr. Collins said suddenly. He rose from his chair and began stalking down one of the classroom aisles. He approached Will's desk.

Uh-oh, Cornelia thought. I've got a bad feeling about this.

"So," Mr. Collins continued, "I've decided to give you a healthy review. Will? Can you remind us what life was like in the Middle Ages?"

"Me?" Will squeaked. She'd still been pulling her notebook and pencils from her backpack when Mr. Collins had suddenly alighted by her desk. She was completely unprepared to be in the teacher's spotlight.

"You already quizzed me in class yester-day," Will murmured.

"I know," Mr. Collins replied breezily. "But, as Mr. Lipsitz pointed out, I'm in a bad mood today."

"I—I don't remember the part about the Middle Ages," Will stuttered nervously. "It's been a long time."

"Uh-huh," Mr. Collins replied. This time, the sarcasm in his voice had a new, hostile edge to it. "You talk about time with a history teacher. Clever."

The mischievous glint returned to Mr. Collins's eyes. Then he shrugged and said to Will, "Let's do it like this. *We'll* move on to the Renaissance period, while *you* spend the next few days writing a report on the state of man during the Middle Ages!"

"Do you know what I have to say to that, Mr. Collins?" Will spat. Her upper lip curled in anger and her forehead was furrowed. "Forget it!" she snapped, in a completely un-Will way.

Something was up. Will had completely lost her cool—something Cornelia never allowed herself. Not in school, anyway!

It was a good thing Will *wasn't* in school at the moment. History class had let out hours ago. Now, Will was on her lunch break, lolling on the Sheffield Institute lawn with her fellow Guardians and regaling them with the tale of her unjust treatment in history class.

"Whoa!" Irma breathed in awe. Hay Lin's and Taranee's eyes widened as they munched on their sandwiches. "Will! You said that to Mr. Collins and he didn't hurl you out of class?"

Will hung her head.

"Actually . . . I really just replied, 'Yes, Mr. Collins,'" she said regretfully. "*But*, you should have heard my tone when I said it!"

Cornelia stifled a smirk. It was true. Will's wild ways had gone no further than a late arrival at history class and a response full of attitude. When Mr. Collins had announced his brutal homework assignment, Will was completely cowed.

"Cornelia," Will said to her with hurt eyes. "You saw the way he attacked me."

Cornelia nodded.

"I have to admit," Cornelia agreed. "He doesn't usually punish people so harshly."

"That should prove something," Will said. She ignored her own lunch as she fumed. "Collins can't be normal. I mean, remember Mrs. Rudolph? She came from Metamoor, too!"

How could Cornelia forget? One moment, Mrs. Rudolph had been an ordinary math teacher—a plodding, portly, seemingly innocent woman. The next thing they knew, she had been transformed into a creature from Metamoor, who looked like a cross between a dreadlocked beach bum and a rhinoceros! She'd insisted to the girls that she was on Metamoor's good team. But Elyon, in one of her visits to the Guardians, had insisted that Mrs. Rudolph was a traitor. The Guardians had no idea whom they could trust. So, at the moment, they trusted no one.

That didn't mean, however, that they were going to start accusing a completely *new* set of suspects of inner scaliness!

"Come on, *another* monster?" Cornelia asked Will skeptically. "And you're only feeling it now? Don't you think it's possible that you just have something personal against Mr. Collins?"

Will's eyes flashed.

"Are you saying I'm making all this up?" she screeched at Cornelia.

Smelling a hint of strife in the air, the other girls stopped munching.

"I'm only saying," Cornelia said, as delicately as she could, "that maybe you *believe* you had that fainting spell. Maybe—"

"Stop!" Will barked, slamming her fists down. "Don't say anything else."

She scanned the rest of the group.

"Do you think Cornelia's right?" she asked softly.

Cornelia felt a prickle of panic on the back of her neck.

Oh, no, she thought. Just when we were beginning to get along, Will has to go all super-sensitive on me.

But at least the other girls saw her side of things.

"Come on, Will," Hay Lin said sweetly. "You have to admit, it's a strange coincidence."

"And you *have* already said," Taranee pointed out, "that Mr. Collins is a spy for your mother. . . . That your mom's all worried about your grades."

Even Irma reluctantly got on board.

"I don't usually agree with Cornelia," she announced, "but this time . . ."

"You know what?" Will said, hanging her head and lurching to her feet. "I've gotta go."

Will turned and began plodding toward Sheffield's front gate. She seemed to have forgotten that the girls had a whole afternoon of classes left.

She's also forgotten that we Guardians are on the same team, Cornelia thought indignantly. The moment there's even an ounce of disagreement, she bails. Maybe she's not such a leader after all!

The other girls looked less annoyed than chagrined. In fact, Taranee looked as knotted up as one of her tight braids.

"Will!" she called after her friend. "Wait!"

"Taranee," Cornelia said quietly. "You need to just let her go."

"But she's upset!" Taranee protested.

"No," Cornelia stated. "She's confused. We're the Guardians. A lot of strange things are happening to us. But that doesn't mean we have to see danger—and Metamoorians—*everywhere*."

Even as Cornelia said it, she felt a twinge in her gut. Was what she had said true?

She shook her head in annoyance.

Great, she thought ruefully. Another nasty change in my world. I used to be so sure of myself. I knew what I liked and what I didn't. I knew what was right and what was wrong, who was an Infielder, and who was an Outfielder.

Then along comes Will Vandom—and a bunch of superpowers I never asked for—and suddenly I don't know which end is up!

THREE

Mr. Collins stood on the edge of the Sheffield Institute's wide lawn and crossed his arms over his thin chest. His breath flowed into his lungs—feeble things—with a faint, wheezing noise. His body felt weak, ineffectual . . . old!

The scene he was witnessing on the other side of the grass, however, perked him right up.

Will Vandom was lurching to her feet and staring down at a quartet of her little friends. Even though Mr. Collins was too far away to see Will's big, brown eyes, her body language communicated everything he needed to know.

Her shoulders were hunched beneath her ears—an especially annoying nervous habit, Mr. Collins thought. She pointed accusingly at the most elegant girl in the group—

Cornelia. And then she began to trudge away.

Cutting class, Will? Mr. Collins wondered with a low, snarky laugh. Okay, let's just add that to the list of blights on your day.

With that thought, Mr. Collins began to pad lightly across the grass. He didn't worry about all the students lounging under trees and tossing Frisbees. He was a teacher, which meant he was invisible. Mr. Collins rounded a corner of the looming main building and approached a smaller structure—the old administration quarters—nestled among a thicket of overgrown shrubs.

He breezed through the front door and glanced around. Half-empty paint cans were scattered on a tarpaulin, and a ladder led up to the exposed ductwork in the ceiling. A band of striped, plastic tape blocked off a dramatic, marble staircase.

Mr. Collins sneered at the blockade, then marched over to the stairs. With one finger, he lifted the tape to shoulder height. He was just ducking beneath it when a guttural voice rang out behind him.

"Mr. Collins!"

The teacher straightened up and growled in

annoyance. He forced a tight smile onto his face, and turned around.

A stout man in white coveralls and a dirty baseball cap was hurrying toward him. It was Bertold, one of the school custodians.

And a big busybody, Mr. Collins thought. Everywhere I go, it seems, there's Bertold. The guy really gets around for someone so pudgy!

"Don't you know this side of the school is closed for repairs?" the janitor demanded of Mr. Collins.

"Of course I know," Mr. Collins replied with a jovial laugh. "You already told me that, this morning."

Then Mr. Collins leaned over to peer directly into Bertold's eyes. His smile hardened as he added, "And as you did this morning, you will now forget you ever saw me!"

With a sigh of satisfaction, Mr. Collins watched the custodian's dull, brown eyes grow even duller. His lids grew heavy and his mouth slackened. In a monotone, Bertold said, "Yes, sir. I'll go now, sir."

Bertold turned around and walked like a robot down the hall.

Mr. Collins tweaked his mustache and

slipped beneath the tape, striding up the stairs. He glanced over his shoulder and sneered at Bertold's back, as the man trundled away.

Earth people, he thought in disdain. Bah! Some minds are too easy to control. But I must admit . . .

Mr. Collins lifted a hand to his shock of thick, brown hair and gave his scalp a vicious rub.

The mind belonging to the *real* Mr. Collins was giving him a rough time.

The man walked briskly through a sun-filled hallway at the top of the stairs and entered a dusky office, a space once occupied by the vice principal.

Sitting in quiet bewilderment at a desk in the corner was Mr. Collins's exact double, from the thick, brown hair to the brushlike mustache to the professorial, blue blazer and tie.

"Collins!" said the "false" Mr. Collins in a loud voice. "Can you hear me?"

From his seat at the desk, the teacher spoke thickly, as if he were half asleep. His voice droned in the same monotone Bertold had assumed after having been hypnotized.

"Yes," he murmured.

"The break has ended," the false Mr. Collins declared. He strode over to the real Mr. Collins's desk and planted his hands on the surface, leaning over to glare into eyes exactly like his own.

"When you go back to your classroom," the false Mr. Collins ordered, "you won't remember anything. Clear?"

"Yes."

The teacher lurched out of his chair and shuffled foggily out of the office.

The false Mr. Collins dusted off his hands and sighed with relief. But as he got ready to get back to his *own* work, he paused.

I think I'll watch him for a minute, he thought.

Grinning slyly, he silently followed the hapless history teacher down the hallway. Then he hid behind a corner to watch the real Mr. Collins walk down the staircase and duck beneath the security tape.

And, of course, there, again, was that bumbler, Bertold, sweeping up paint chips at the base of the stairs! He looked at the real Mr. Collins disapprovingly.

"Professor!" he scolded. "Even if construction has been stopped, this side of the school is still forbidden to the public."

The real Mr. Collins nodded agreeably and headed for the door. Behind him, Bertold leaned on his broom and said, "Why do I have the feeling I've already told you this?"

Slowly, the real Mr. Collins turned around. He shook his head, as if he had been trying to knock cobwebs out of his brain, and shrugged.

"Maybe it's déjà vu, Bertold," he said.

Then he shook his head again . . . and looked around the dusty old foyer.

"Now that you mention it," he breathed in confusion. "I'm a bit confused, too. What . . . what am I doing here?"

While the befuddled teacher shambled from the building, the man spying on him from the top of the stairs gave a low, satisfied cackle.

Neither Bertold nor Mr. Collins had remembered a thing, he confirmed to himself gleefully. Not that he didn't have absolute faith in his own powers. He just liked to see them in action every once in a while.

Speaking of which . . . he thought as he turned back into the hallway. It's time to take a little restorative action for myself.

Standing in front of a window, the man gazed at his own reflection. He smirked at himself in the glass, then gave a quick nod.

A silvery shimmer surrounded his body, thrumming and roiling like a sudden burst of steam. As the magic melted away, so, too, did the irritating, brushlike mustache, the bland, friendly face, the rounded shoulders, and the practical suit.

In their place appeared long, flowing, blond hair and a jawline so sharp it could cut paper. The eyes, still leering, had morphed from hazel to icy blue. They squinted in a sinister smile.

Ah, Cedric thought in relief. That's it. I can work much better this way!

Now in a more comfortable form, he stalked back down the hallway and swept down the stairs. He had to get to the bookshop. It was the only place where he could find peace. And where he could enact the next leg of his plan.

Minutes later, Cedric was in the bookshop. Once inside, he breathed in the musty, dusty air with relish.

Oh, but it wasn't the shelves filled with old books that brought Cedric comfort. Or the warm shafts of rainbow sunlight that shot through the elegant, stained-glass windows. No, it was the bookshop's proximity to his home—to Metamoor. The building housed a portal to Cedric's world.

And waiting for him there was Prince Phobos. Just the thought of Phobos—his power, his fury, his chiseled face and long, wheat-colored hair—made Cedric shudder. He didn't know whether he admired the prince as much as he feared him.

The moment such a thought entered Cedric's mind, he shook it away. Such disloyalty was inexcusable! Phobos was his ruler. Cedric served him unconditionally. That was all. And if the prince's cruelty caused Cedric pain, he would just have to deal with it on his own. It certainly was something that had to be kept hidden from Elyon. Nothing must dissuade her from forsaking her "parents" and friends for her brother, Phobos. And nothing could be allowed to sway her faith in Cedric's power.

The same went for Vathek. The big, blue lug had been endlessly loyal to Cedric.

And now, Cedric thought, my trust in the

monster will be put to the test. Let's see if he's up to the task.

Cedric strode through the shop to a door made of yellowed, frosted glass. Opening the door with magic—there was no reason to soil his own hands—Cedric stepped into a small back office and approached an ornate, gold lectern. Atop the stand was an ancient book. Its leather cover was crinkled with age and dirt.

Flipping open the book, Cedric waved a casual hand over the pages. A wisp of magic trailed from his fingertips and danced lightly over the parchment. Then the wisp pulled backward, as if teasing a thread loose from a sweater.

What emerged from the book, however, was much more interesting than a slip of string. It was a magical vision-cloud—a hazy screen through which Cedric could see, and talk to, his aide back in Metamoor.

With another flick of his magical finger, Cedric summoned Vathek. The beast's head emerged in the cloud as clearly as an earthly being might appear in a video monitor. Vathek, who viewed Cedric's image through a translucent jewel in one of his brass wrist cuffs, bowed his bulbous head reverently.

Cedric cleared his throat to deepen his voice. Then he spoke.

"Talk to me, faithful Vathek," he intoned. "Tell me how things are going."

"Well, Cedric," Vathek responded. "I've entered Metamoor's underground and infiltrated the rebels who long to escape to earth. I told them that I betrayed you."

"Go on," Cedric urged.

"Unfortunately," Vathek admitted, "some don't believe me. So now they are divided. Those who fell for my trick are now under my orders."

"Really," Cedric said drily. "I didn't know you were so charismatic, old friend."

Inside, however, Cedric felt a sense of excitement. The plan was working! Phobos would be pleased.

Vathek was speaking once again. Cedric shook himself out of his happiness and returned to the conversation.

"Those on my 'team' are few and desperate," the blue henchman was saying. "They would believe anybody."

"Well, make sure they don't influence you!"

Cedric warned. "Remember whom you must obey."

"I won't forget, my master," Vathek said, from his little cloud. "I only wonder why we must deceive them."

"We're not deceiving them," Cedric said. "We're giving them an actual chance to invade earth. We're even helping them get there without interference! After all, I'm using all my resources to weaken the Guardians."

Vathek flashed a snaggletoothed grin.

"May I ask how?" he inquired.

"First of all," Cedric said, "I'm undermining all the closest relationships of Will, the keeper of the Heart of Candracar. I've got her fighting with her mother and giving the cold shoulder to her friends. It was easy enough to add a little confusion into her life. Before you know it, she'll be useless to her fellow Guardians.

"But," Cedric continued, "I haven't done this alone. Elyon will supply the finishing stroke."

Vathek nodded enthusiastically.

"And so the plan will take place tonight?" he inquired.

"Yes, Vathek," Cedric said. "Instill rage in

your followers. Teach them to distrust the Guardians."

As Cedric issued his final orders, he felt another thrill of excitement shoot through his veins. Deceit. Destruction. And most of all, pleasing Phobos—it really did warm his heart!

"Yes," Cedric repeated slyly. "We'll leave the rebels the task of destroying our pesky Guardians—destroying them with their rage!"

FOUR

Will turned her back on her friends, blocking out their troubled, skeptical faces.

She trudged out Sheffield's front gate.

And then she headed for the school's bike rack. She'd unlocked her red bike and begun pedaling away before she fully realized what she was doing. Because what she was doing was totally ditching school! This was a first in the history of Will Vandom—eternal good girl, follower of rules, Guardian without a clue.

Of course, Will thought drily, being anointed to save the world is a first, too.

And here was another—having her friends totally turn on her! Will couldn't believe they'd been so dismissive of her Mr. Collins–is–evil theory.

They don't know what it feels like, Will thought, to walk by a Metamoorian and think you're gonna have your head explode. Morosely, she pedaled down the street, leaving Sheffield's bustling, laughter-filled, lunchtime scene far behind her.

And they don't know what it feels like to be the group's fifth wheel, Will said to herself as a lump rose in her throat. They're earth, air, fire, and water. Cornelia, Hay Lin, Taranee, and Irma fit together like peas in a pod. Meanwhile, I'm the odd Guardian out. What am I doing here?

At that thought, Will let a little sob escape her throat. She'd thought she belonged in their clique. She'd even started to feel comfortable in Heatherfield. But she'd been wrong. She was an outsider.

A mopey, school-skipping outsider at that!

I *hate* Heatherfield, Will thought, giving her bike bell a vicious tweak. It twanged in off-key protest.

I didn't want to come here, Will thought. And my mother knew it all along. Standing up on her bike pedals, Will climbed a short hill. When she reached the top, she could see a swath of annoyingly beautiful buildings; a wrought-iron fence guarding a charming park; and . . . sitting on the curb with a guitar at his feet . . . a boy.

But not just any boy! It was Matt—Will's sweet-eyed crush. He was the only thing that made Heatherfield bearable at that moment.

"Hello!" Will chirped, braking at Matt's feet with a breathless skid. "What are you doing here?"

Matt unfolded his long, lanky limbs to stand up and smile at Will.

Ohhhhh, Will thought tremulously. So tall. So cute!

"I'm on the afternoon schedule at school," Matt explained. "What about you? Aren't you supposed to be at Sheffield, right now?"

"Well . . . I . . ." Will couldn't even begin to wrap her brain around the proper Matt-impressing strategy. Would he think cutting class was cool? Or should she protect her good-girl rep and tell him she had had a doctor's appointment? Or should she just keep staring up into his chocolaty-brown eyes?

"Hey, Matt!"

It looked as though the answer was to be

none of the above. At the sound of a guy's voice bellowing his name, Matt looked away from Will and peeked over his shoulder. A trio of scruffy dudes with guitars and drums slung over their shoulders were gazing at Matt expectantly. Will recognized them—they were the other members of Cobalt Blue, Matt's band.

His very cool band, Will thought, in which he plays lead guitar and sings. *Sighhhhh.*

"Come on, man," the goateed bass player shouted. "You're the only one missing."

"Coming," Matt called out. Then he turned back to Will with an apologetic shrug.

"Sorry," he said. "The boys in the band are waiting. We're gonna go try out for a gig at Sheffield!"

Will felt her head nod up and down enthusiastically. It felt strangely detached from her body, for some reason. But she was glad it—her head, that is—had taken the lead and was responding to Matt with appropriate gestures. That left Will's brain free to imagine herself holding hands with Matt.

And going to the movies with Matt.

And kissing Ma—

"I'll see you later, okay?" Matt was saying.

Will came crashing back to reality.

Earth to Crush Girl, she said to herself. He's talking to you!

She nodded and gave Matt a little wave.

"Sure, no problem," she said. "Go ahead."

He went—running over to join his buds. When he reached them, the bass player grabbed the hood of Matt's gray sweatshirt and yanked it playfully over his shaggy, brown hair. Then he dragged Matt down the sidewalk while Matt struggled against him, guffawing loudly.

He's *soooo* mature, Will thought, gazing after her crush. If he liked me, I mean really liked me, *then* I'd have a good reason to stay in Heatherfield.

When, and only when, Matt had disappeared over the hill, Will sighed and climbed back onto her bike. Then, wistfully, she made her way slowly home.

Walking through the door of the breezy loft she shared with her mom, she looked around. Just the other day, they'd finally finished unpacking all of the boxes after their move. Mom had arranged the cushy, red couch and bookshelves into a welcoming room. And she'd baked chocolate-chip cookies—the scent still hung in the air. The place was *almost* beginning to feel homey to Will.

It helped that she had a pet to greet her at the door. The moment Will stepped inside the loft, her little dormouse came running toward her. It wrinkled its nose at Will happily, its fluffy tail bobbing with excitement.

"Hey," Will said. "How did you manage to get out of my bedroom?"

Will usually kept her critter locked in her room during the day. It tended to make nests out of *anything* soft, and it had an uncanny knack for worming its way into the cookie jar. To say it was a nuisance was an understatement.

But today, Will was glad to see the doormouse. It jumped into her arms, then quickly scampered onto her shoulders.

"I actually didn't feel like coming home today," Will admitted to the dormouse. It nosed at her cheek with a little squeak. "After all, all my problems started here. But where else am I supposed to go? I don't feel like seeing *anybody*!"

Will flopped onto the couch. The jolt sent the dormouse bouncing onto her head! She waited for it to jump off again, but the animal seemed to like it up there. So Will shrugged and glanced at the answering machine, which sat on a buffet table behind the couch. Its red light was blinking. Will reached for the PLAY button.

"I bet it's a message from Mom," she sighed. Then she assumed her mother's grown-up voice and mimicked, "'Hello honey! I'll be back late again tonight. Keep your cell phone on so I can find you. Blah, blah, blah . . .'"

Rolling her eyes, Will pressed the button.

"*Beeeeeep* . . . It's me, honey!" Mom's voice echoed from the machine. "I'll be late tonight. But I'll be bringing something home for dinner. So, keep your cell phone on and—"

Will cut off the rest of her mother's message with a jab at the pause button. Then she shot her dormouse a smug smile.

"Did you hear that?" she crowed. "I was so right. Okay, let's see if there are any more surprises on here."

Will sped through her mom's message and hit PLAY again. Now, a new voice piped out of the machine. And this one made Will jump.

"Hello, Will," trilled a young woman. "It's

51

Vera! I have some great news for you. Come on down to the pool when you can!"

"Yes! My new swim coach," Will cried. "That's all I need to hear!"

She jumped off the couch, sending the dormouse scampering for footing. Its claws dug into the fabric of the cherry-red couch. But Will didn't have time to reprimand it. She had someplace to be.

I'll get my swim bag and head over to the pool right now, she thought as she ran out of the room. "Swimming helps me think, anyway," she added breathlessly.

Only a few seconds later, Will was heading for the door, her orange mesh swim bag bouncing at her side. She waved to the dormouse, which was still scampering around on the couch and sniffing at the answering machine. She had just played a few messages for her mom and was now nearing the end of its voice mail queue.

"Off I go," Will announced to the dormouse. "See ya! Don't break anything!"

As Will flounced happily out of the loft, she thought she heard her mother's voice, echoing out of the answering machine once again. Out of habit, she started to pause and to listen carefully.

But then she remembered that she and her mom were feuding. Which meant Mom's message could just wait!

Even if that message were: "It's Mom again. I forgot to mention one thing—I love you!"

The words half registered in Will's fretful mind. But then she shook her head and imagined herself diving into the warm, welcoming blue water of Sheffield's indoor swimming pool. Decisively, she turned from the door and headed down the hall.

She had someplace to be. Maybe she'd feel like giving Mom's voice mail a more thoughtful listen later.

FIVE

After Will left them on the Sheffield lawn, the remaining Guardians blinked at each other in surprise. Talk about a meltdown!

Nobody was more troubled by Will's tantrum than Hay Lin. If Haylin had learned anything from her grandmother before she had passed away, it was that the Guardians had to stick together.

Hay Lin's grandmother knew that rule better than anyone. All of Hay Lin's life, her grandmother had filled her head with stories, from ancient Chinese fables to tales of ancient Greek philosophers. She'd also urged her granddaughter to believe in magic.

Hay Lin's parents had thought the old woman was simply eccentric. Now, Hay Lin knew the truth—her grandmother had once been a Guardian herself! And when the Oracle had decided that Hay Lin and her friends would take up the saving-the-world torch, it had been her grandmother who had told them all about their new powers and responsibilities. She had also given Hay Lin a magical map of Heatherfield, one that pointed out the location of Metamoorian portals.

Hay Lin wondered what her grandmother was thinking as Will stalked away from the group—for she was sure Grandma was peeking down at them from Candracar. Did her grandmother fear that W.i.t.c.h. was falling apart?

Or was she nodding knowingly and saying, "Silly girls. I remember when I squabbled with my fellow Guardians. We were making up over tea and cookies within an hour."

I'm gonna go with that second scenario, Hay Lin thought with a firm nod as the early bell rang. Her grin restored, Hay Lin popped to her feet and threw away the dregs of her lunch—dumplings and sesame noodles left over from her parents' Chinese restaurant. Then she grabbed her pink backpack and followed her friends into the school.

The moment they arrived in the crowded hallway, the warning bell rang above their heads. Cornelia gave her friends a wave and hurried off to her class. She hated to be late.

Irma and Taranee, on the other hand, lingered in the hallway with Hay Lin for a moment. Their math class, after all, was only steps away and their substitute teacher was nowhere to be seen yet.

Bells, bells, bells, Hay Lin thought happily. Ever since my new power arrived, they sound like much more than noisy things herding us into our classrooms. These bells are filled with dozens of gossip sessions and a symphony of locker slams. With millions of memories.

That about summed up Hay Lin's new magic. Any sound she heard sent scenes from the past flashing through her mind. She'd first discovered the ability when the girls were sneaking around Mrs. Rudolph's house, searching for portals and clues.

The moment Hay Lin had happened upon an old music box in Mrs. Rudolph's hallway, she had gotten a blast from the past. In her mind, she'd seen Mrs. Rudolph in her scaly Metamoorian form. She'd been crossing through a portal from Metamoor to earth. And she hadn't been alone. With her had been a couple and an infant. Hay Lin now knew that they had been Elyon and her parents—the people everyone had believed to be Elyon's parents, anyway.

Whether Hay Lin had been witnessing baby Elyon's rescue or a kidnapping was unclear.

But one thing Hay Lin did know—her new power was amazing! Even when it came to her through the ringling of yet another bell. This one was the "Get to class, now. I mean it!" bell.

Of course, Hay Lin's friends weren't nearly as enamored of the sound as she was.

"Yikes!" Irma squealed, clapping her hands over her ears.

"Yeah, yeah, we're going, already!" Taranee complained, glaring up at the bell.

"Actually, I think it's quite a nice bit of music," Hay Lin said with a smile.

"You call *that* music?" Irma gasped, as Taranee hurried over with an awed expression on her face. She glanced around at the kids dashing to class. When she was sure nobody was eavesdropping, she said to Hay Lin, "You can use your power on that off-key bell?"

"I can do it selectively," Hay Lin explained, with a happy shrug. "Every melody is linked to a certain memory, and I get to feel it."

"Melody," Irma scoffed, shaking her head.

"For example . . ." Hay Lin began. She closed her eyes, letting an image that had been hazy a moment ago clarify itself in her mind. "That bell brought me a memory of a boy who loved walking down these halls."

Then Hay Lin cocked her head. She was envisioning something else! Something in the dying echo of students' footsteps, shuffling to their classrooms. The sound was so enticing, she couldn't help dropping to her hands and knees for a better listen.

"Even the sound of footsteps in the hall is distinct," she whispered to Irma and Taranee. They stood behind her, breathlessly waiting to hear what memory Hay Lin would come up with next.

"Do you hear it?" Hay Lin continued, bending her head and frowning in concentration. "The footsteps are light. Hesitant. I remember . . ."

"Mrs. Rudolph!" Irma squealed from her spot behind Hay Lin.

"You think so?" Hay Lin asked, listening harder and squeezing her eyes shut. "I'm actually thinking it's Bertold, the janitor."

When Hay Lin got no response, she peeked over her shoulder. That's when she realized Irma and Taranee hadn't been reminiscing about Mrs. Rudolph! They'd been looking right at her!

The teacher—whom the Guardians had last seen in Metamoor, in her armor of brown scales and dreadlocks—was back in her plump, human guise. She was wearing a cardigan sweater, a green scarf, and oversized spectacles. She looked every bit the math teacher. With a smile, she walked toward the girls.

"Wow!" Hay Lin whispered to her friends. "It's really her!"

"Why are you looking at me that way?" Mrs. Rudolph asked slyly as she came to a halt in front of the girls. "I'm back from my vacation. Is that such a big surprise?"

"Yes!" Irma retorted, glaring at the teacher and placing her fists on her hips. "Did you rest enough in *Metamoor*?"

"Don't be so suspicious," Mrs. Rudolph scoffed. "Have you forgotten that I saved your life in Metamoor?"

Then she turned to Taranee and gave her a kind smile. Taking the stunned girl's chin in her hand, she said, "And you, Taranee. I'm glad to see you're well!"

"Th—thank you," Taranee replied, looking confused.

But Irma wasn't going to let Mrs. Rudolph off so easy.

"Tell us the truth," she said. "You don't belong in this world. Why did you come back?"

"To save you again," Mrs. Rudolph replied. "I couldn't leave you in the hands of that substitute teacher."

Hay Lin put a hand over her mouth to suppress a snort of laughter. Mrs. Rudolph was almost . . . cool! Cool, that is, for a math-teacher-turned-monster who just might be the Guardians' enemy.

"Jokes aside," Mrs. Rudolph continued, glancing at Hay Lin with a smile in her eyes, "when you discovered my true nature, I had to escape. In your eyes, I looked monstrous. And when something frightens human beings, they tend to destroy the cause of the fear."

Hay Lin shot her friends a guilty look. There was no denying what Mrs. Rudolph had said.

That which was foreign was frightening, whether it came in the form of Outfielders at school or talking lizards from Metamoor.

"But now," Mrs. Rudolph said, cutting short Hay Lin's guilt trip, "I really think we could help one another."

"How?" Irma demanded.

Mrs. Rudolph glanced around the empty hallway.

"The school is not the right place to talk about this," she said. "Why don't you all come to my house this afternoon for tea and cookies?"

Tea and cookies! Hay Lin thought. Just as Grandma said in my daydream. It must be a sign. So, though Taranee and Irma continued to look skeptical, Hay Lin nodded.

The girls followed Mrs. Rudolph into the classroom and hurried to their seats. The teacher settled into her seat at the front of the room.

"Good morning, everyone," she announced. "Quiet down. As I was telling some of your classmates, I've taken a vacation. . . ."

Blah, blah, blah, Hay Lin thought. I've gotta admit, I kind of liked having the substitute teacher. She was a breeze. And even if Mrs. Rudolph is an impostor, she's a really good one. Her algebra homework always is pretty tough. And her return means it's back to the grind.

Mrs. Rudolph started the lesson—something about binomials. Yawn! But, mindful of her grade, Hay Lin did her best to listen.

The only problem? Another voice was echoing in her head! A voice that sounded a lot like Taranee's!

Hay Lin glanced at her friend. Taranee wasn't whispering. In fact, she was staring down at her notebook in rapt concentration.

But Hay Lin was sure she could hear Taranee's voice, reedy, whispery, but distinct, in her brain.

Irma! Taranee was saying. *Can you hear me?*

Taranee! Irma's voice replied. Hay Lin peeked at Irma. Her friend's eyes were sparkling with delight and surprise. But, like Taranee's, her lips were motionless. *Are you communicating with me mentally?*

Yes! Taranee replied, grinning at her friend. *And you're answering. Will and I discovered this power when I was in Metamoor. I wanted to test it out with you.*

Are you saying, Irma gasped in Hay Lin's mind, *we can talk and nobody can hear us?*

Uh-huh! Taranee responded. *Now I'll try to contact Hay Lin, too!*

I hear you, girls! Hay Lin thought.

One glance at Irma and Taranee, smiling at her in glee, told her that they'd heard her.

This is absolutely better than note-passing, Hay Lin communicated to her girlfriends with a giggle.

Listen, Taranee said. *I can't keep the mental link for long. So, what should we do? Do we go to Mrs. Rudolph's tonight?*

I don't know, Irma replied. *She's too suspicious! I don't trust her!*

I say let's go, Hay Lin said with a shrug. She glanced over at Mrs. Rudolph to be sure her teacher couldn't see the girls making eye contact. The woman seemed immersed in the math lesson.

I'm curious, Hay Lin continued.

All right, Irma replied reluctantly. *But only with Will and Cornelia. Without them, I won't go back inside that house. No way!*

Good idea, Hay Lin thought. *Especially where Will is concerned. I'm worried about her. Hey!*

Hay Lin saw both Irma and Taranee jump.

Whoops! she thought, giving her friends an apologetic smile. *I guess even silent communication has a volume control.*

Anyway, she continued, *can you contact Will, Taranee? We could ask her right now!*

Only by phone, Taranee said. *She's too far away. This power of mine is still limited. But you're right. The last thing we want is to find out that Cedric is behind Mrs. Rudolph's strange behavior, manipulating things with his deceit and lies.*

No, Taranee continued, her voice echoing eerily in Hay Lin's head now. It was getting more wispy and ghostly. In a moment, Hay Lin felt sure, Taranee's magic would give out. The girls would be left to note-passing and, ugh, paying attention to their algebra lesson. *We need to go to Mrs. Rudolph's as a team,* Taranee thought.

The last thing Hay Lin heard before Taranee's thoughts quieted, leaving Hay Lin with a strangely hollow feeling in her head, was, *We need Will!*

SIX

Will swam down her lane of the pool, feeling the water skim over her body with each kick.

Ah, the freestyle, she thought.

It was her favorite stroke. It made her feel powerful and free and completely weightless. It made her want to stay in that chlorine-scented haven forever.

I have plenty of other reasons to hide here, Will thought, before plunging upside down to execute a perfect flip-turn. Wouldn't it be nice to never again have to deal with my nagging mother and my doubting friends, not to mention all those big, surly creatures from Metamoor?

The only person, Will thought, as she began to whiz through another lap, I would actually like to see would be—

"Have you decided to train yourself, Will?"

At the sound of a bubbly voice, Will popped her head out of the water. It was Vera! She was standing at the end of Will's lane, grinning down at her. Will sped to the wall at the end of her lane and hoisted herself halfway out of the water.

"Hi, Vera!" she chirped. "I got your message."

"Yes, but I thought I told you we'd start training *after* school," Vera said with a kind smile. "Not during. What would your mother say if she found out you were here?"

"I know," Will said, pulling the swim cap off her head gloomily. "I've never skipped class before. But . . ."

Will's voice trailed off as she remembered who she was talking to. Vera may have been sweet and pretty and younger than most of the adults in Will's world. But she was still a swim coach. That was practically a teacher!

". . . I had to do it," Will finished weakly, sure that Vera was going to reprimand her.

She gave Vera a fearful, sidelong glance. But instead of whipping out a demerit book or glaring at her and hissing, *"Truant,"* Vera merely smiled sympathetically.

"Want to talk about it?" she asked.

A half hour later, Will was lounging in Heatherfield's newest coffeehouse. It was a sun-filled, mod space with floor-to-ceiling windows and candy-colored, molded, plastic furniture. The scent of cinnamon-spiked espresso wafted pleasantly beneath Will's nose as she watched Vera lean against the front counter. A tousled-haired waiter was handing her a couple of cups of steaming hot coffee.

"Two cappuccinos, Vera," he announced.

"Thanks, Bill," the coach burbled in reply. "You're the best!"

When Vera rejoined Will at their window-side table, Will took a slurp of the sweet, milky coffee, and she looked around happily.

"This is a nice café," she said.

"Yes," Vera nodded. She pointed at Bill, who was frothing up some mochas—*and* giving Vera sidelong looks. "And the waiter isn't so bad, either!"

"Vera!" Will giggled into her cappuccino foam. "What are you saying?"

"That there are a lot of people in the world besides your four friends and Matt!" Vera declared with an exaggerated yawn.

"In the *world*, maybe," Will agreed. "But in Heatherfield . . ."

"Listen to me," Vera said, reaching across their orange table to place her hand on top of Will's. "Don't waste your time with that guy Matt. You deserve something better!"

Was Vera proposing that she simply discard her crush like a stack of junk mail? Even if she wanted to, how could she ever get that strong, scruffy chin and those warm, brown eyes out of her head?

"Matt means a lot to me," Will protested. "Even . . . if he doesn't really know it."

Hearing how pathetic her own words sounded, Will's shoulders slumped. Vera's scoffing didn't help matters.

"Listen to yourself," Vera said. "You're day-dreaming about the wrong guy!"

While Will squirmed uncomfortably in her slick chair, Vera moved on to an even touchier subject.

"As for your friends," she said, "you still haven't told me why you had a fight."

As Vera took a sip of coffee and gazed at Will with inquisitive blue eyes, Will bit her lip. She had to tread carefully there. No matter how much she might have trusted Vera, she still couldn't let her in on the group's secret. *Nobody* could be told the truth. The loss of their anonymity would put a serious damper on their war with the Metamoorians.

Just the thought of exposure made Will very nervous. She found herself speaking with exaggerated care.

"My friends and I . . . had a difference of opinion," she told Vera. "Especially me and Cornelia. She'd love to be the leader of our group."

"So you let her," Vera offered casually. She leaned back in her seat and smiled, just as Bill approached their table with a plate of croissants. Sending the waiter a flirty glance, Vera said to Will, "Let your friend Cornelia take what she wants. At your age, it's easy to make new friends."

For a moment—just a moment—Will let himself imagine such a thing. Saying goodbye to her friends, and to their increasingly daunting idea, gave her a second of relief.

But an instant later, that relief was replaced by a terrible pang. Never dishing with Taranee again? Never being able to hear about Irma's latest flirtation? Viewing Hay Lin's far-out fashion only from a distance?

Will shook her head. The idea was unthinkable.

"I can't walk away from my friends," Will insisted to Vera. She let out a big sigh. "There's . . . well, something big that links us."

If you only knew *how* big, Will thought ruefully. She gazed into her coffee cup, afraid her eyes would betray her anxious thoughts.

Luckily, Vera had moved on to a new topic.

"Hey," she said with a shrug. "Do what you've gotta do. But let's get to the reason I called you—to talk about your swimming in the All-State Championship!"

"Really?" Will squealed, jumping out of her seat. "Yahoo!"

Every eye in the coffeehouse swiveled toward Will.

Uh, did I just scream and yell in the middle of a crowded coffeehouse? Will thought, feeling herself turn red. Maybe Cornelia's right. Leadership *has* gone to my head.

But Will was too happy to get all angsty about her gaffe. She merely flopped back into her seat and gazed at Vera with incredulity.

"That's fantastic news!" she said to the beaming swim coach. "Of course, my mother won't take it well."

"She'll have to," Vera said, breezy as ever. "It's official. You're representing our school at the championship. I'll talk to your mom."

Vera reached across the table to grab Will's hand again.

"She'll change her mind when she sees what you can do."

"Oh, Vera," Will sighed happily. "You're too good to be true!"

Already, images of herself were forming in Will's mind. She saw herself climbing onto the starting block in front of a throng of screaming fans. Hearing a buzzer blare as she touched the wall first. Climbing onto a medal stand and bowing her head to receive her reward.

Of course, her fantasy didn't last long; soon, unavoidable reality intruded. Guardian duties had already stretched Will's study schedule too thin. How was she going to add extra practice time on top of all that?

"Do you honestly think," Will asked Vera, "that I can study and train at the same time?"

She couldn't hide the shakiness in her voice. With each passing second, elation was giving way to apprehension.

But Vera waved Will's fears away with the same life-is-a-breeze bubbliness she always showed.

"Certainly," she declared. "It's only a question of organizing your schedule. Speaking of which, you should probably hit the road, huh?"

Will glanced at her watch. Dinnertime was fast approaching, and she still had to deal with Mr. Collins's odious assignment!

"Yeah," she admitted. "I just have to get my bag from the locker room."

"Go on," Vera said. She glanced at the stuff scattered on the table. Among the crumpled napkins and croissant crumbs were her clipboard and Will's date book and cell phone. "Leave your stuff here. I'll guard it."

Will flashed Vera another grateful smile and popped out of her chair. As she darted to the closet in the front of the café, where she'd checked her backpack, she felt so light on her feet she almost thought she could fly!

The feeling made Will pause in concern. Apprehensively, she glanced over her shoulder. She sighed with relief when she saw that her back was still just that—an unadorned back.

Whew, she thought. For a moment there, I thought I'd sprouted my wings!

Luckily, Will was still undercover. In fact, she felt as though her luck were changing all around! With Vera on her side, she felt as though there were nothing she couldn't do!

SEVEN

Vera watched Will jump up from their table and dash to the coat check. The girl was practically skipping!

Ah, Vera thought, I remember when paltry accomplishments excited me that much. I used to walk on air! Just like Will's doing now.

Memories flooded Vera's mind, and a dreamy expression crept onto her face. But her reverie was short-lived. An annoying *briiip, briiip, briiip* pierced her daydream, deflating it as if it were a balloon.

Ugh, she thought. Her smiling blue eyes narrowed in a squint. That sounds like an electronic cricket. I've always hated crickets. They never shut up!

Vera looked around for the source of the

annoying beeps. It was Will's cell phone! The thing was bleating and vibrating as if the world were coming to an end. Its tiny screen glowed a bright, acid green.

Vera regarded the phone with a cold frown. Then she sneered at the gadget.

"Be quiet, you!" she ordered the phone.

Immediately, the phone obeyed, falling silent with a *bluuurp*. Glancing around to make sure nobody was watching, Vera waved away the wisps of silvery magic that hovered around the phone.

Then she smiled smugly and took a sip of her cappuccino.

Of course, no sooner had she found a moment of peace than something *else* intruded upon it. This time, the invader was no chirping, robotic bug. But it was definitely a pest—in the form of her waiter, Bill! And Bill's flirtiness had evaporated as surely as had the cell phone's batteries. Now he was staring at Vera.

"The girl is right," he said, tucking his coffee tray beneath his arm and storming over to her table. "You *are* too good to be true."

"Ex*cuse* me?" Vera replied. She gazed up at Bill's boyish mop of brown hair and his thin face. Did this dude know who he was dealing with?

Vera gave Bill an indignant, *intimidating* stare.

In response, Bill's eyes flashed. In fact . . . they changed color! Ever so briefly, the waiter's warm, green eyes went icy blue. And he smirked at Vera in an impudent manner that could only belong to . . .

"Cedric!" Vera gasped out loud in recognition. "What are you doing here? Will mustn't see us together!"

"Be quiet," Cedric replied. His eyes returned to their bland, green color and he ran a limp hand through his silky hair. "I'll return the waiter's body to him before Will comes back."

"Are you checking up on me?" Vera asked. "Do you think I can't do this?"

"No," Cedric said. "I just wanted to tell you you're doing a fantastic job."

Vera felt a lightness flutter through her chest. Actually, she had to quell a happy giggle before it escaped her lips! When the surge of joy had passed, she sighed.

Her current body still felt a bit unfamiliar. It often did unexpected things, like breaking into a happy dance when one of her students shattered a personal record. Or almost melting with happiness when her mentor praised her—as he was doing at this very moment.

Cedric (in Bill form) leaned over Vera and put a warm arm around her shoulder. Gently, he turned her in her mod, plastic chair so that they both faced the large windows.

Vera blinked at her reflection. That tall, lithe body and tousled, golden ponytail. That slim face and those sharp collarbones of a woman well into her twenties. Was that . . . really her?

No, of course not. As Bill whispered into her ear, Vera's reflection began to fade. His did, too.

"Thanks to you, my plan is unfolding perfectly," Bill murmured, pointing at their cloudy reflections. At that moment, the images began to come back into focus. Vera stared at her own image.

Well, it wasn't hers *exactly*. While the physical bodies of Bill and Vera remained in the crowded café, the window showed them their true souls.

The waiter's boyish visage had been replaced by Cedric's, with Cedric's sharp cheekbones, waterfall of platinum hair, and fierce, blue eyes.

And Vera's womanly ways? They'd been supplanted by the face and body of a schoolgirl. A girl with wide, wan, blue eyes and straw-colored braids. A girl who hadn't walked around Heatherfeld for quite some time now.

"Yes, you're doing an excellent job," Cedric told the girl. "My bright, skillful, and sly . . . Elyon!"

EIGHT

After giving Vera a grateful hug good-bye, Will went straight to the Sheffield library.

I'll show that Mr. Collins, she thought as she stomped up the steps of the looming, Gothic building. She'd admired the library many times when she'd walked by. It looked like a palace, complete with turrets, cupolas, and a slate roof with dormered windows. Will had always imagined that those dormers were the perfect little nooks for curling up with a good novel.

She'd *had* to imagine it, because this was the first time she'd ever set foot in the library.

I guess I really haven't been the most diligent student, Will thought guiltily as she slipped through the building's tall, front doors. But all that's going to change . . . now?

Will gasped as she looked around. She'd just walked into the most enormous, most intimidating reading room she'd ever seen. The shelves were so tall she could barely see where they ended. Students hunched over huge tomes were arrayed at long, heavy tables. The light was dusky, and the air was stale. The vibe was seriously serious!

A lanky boy with red hair and brown eyes (made googly by his big, round specs) sauntered by. He was wearing a baggy, orange T-shirt and jeans.

"Can I help you find anything?" he asked.

Will, feeling overwhelmed, was thankful for the boy's help. He was a librarian assistant and pointed Will to a section with books about the Middle Ages. The shelves were piled with heavy, old books. "There are so many books!" Will exclaimed.

"I think we have some others in another section. I can bring those to you if you want." the library assistant was being very nice and attentive.

"Thanks," Will said. "I really appreciate it."

Grabbing a few of the large books, Will found an open table and spread her pile of books out. She had lots of reading to do. To write a report on the Middle Ages was no small thing. The thought made Will angry. How could Mr. Collins have done this to her?

And more importantly, how come her friends weren't siding with her?

They seemed to have no use for her theory about Mr. Collins, and they hadn't even tried to stop her when she'd ditched school!

As she replayed the lunchtime scene in her head, Will felt all the elation of her afternoon with Vera begin to drain away.

Should she follow Vera's advice and break away from her friends?

Would the Council of the Congregation even allow her to? Not to mention her conscience!

And what about Matt? Should she find another crush, one who would go so far as to ask her out on an actual date?

The questions were swirling around Will's head so fast she was getting dizzy! And she didn't have a clue as to how to answer them.

Out of the corner of her eye, Will spotted

the library assistant loping toward her. His skinny arms were straining under a stack of leather-bound books.

I never thought I'd be so glad to see that much reading heading my way, Will thought with a sigh. *But I really need the distraction.*

Thudddd!

Will jumped as the boy dumped the pile of books onto the table. Proudly, the lanky guy showed Will what he'd found.

"Life in the Middle Ages," he said, pointing to the first heavy volume in front of Will. *"People of the Dark Years.* And so on and so forth. Everything you need."

Everything? Will thought as she heaved the heavy books onto the table in front of her. *Not even close. But . . . first things first. I'll deal with Mr. Collins's report, and* then *I'll sort out the rest of my life.*

As Will opened *People of the Dark Years*, she realized the boy was still standing there.

"We're closing in three hours," he said. "Are you sure you can manage to read all that?"

"No," Will admitted. "But I can try! Thanks for finding these books!"

"Well, it's my job," the boy said, stuffing his

hands into his pockets and giving Will a sheepish grin. "And I've got a lot of time to spare. . . ."

Will smiled politely, then focused on her book.

I wish *I* had a lot of time, Will muttered to herself as she scanned the first lines of the text. All these books, she thought with a sigh. Some problems obviously can't be solved with magic.

She was soon immersed in her reading. She found a juicy-looking section called "The Landowner and the Serf: A Vicious Disparity." A woodcut illustration above the chapter heading depicted a plump nobleman, wearing puffed sleeves and gnawing on a turkey leg. He was snarling at a group of scrawny workers clustered around his feet.

In Will's mind, the gentleman's fleshy face turned blue. His hair was replaced by rocklike lumps. And the serfs, in their rough, woolen tunics? They grew green tails and forked tongues that flicked at the air nervously.

"*Rich and poor have never been further apart,*" Will read in a whisper, "*than they were in the Dark Ages.*"

Or, Will realized with sudden clarity, than they are in—

"Metamoor!" she exclaimed, jumping to her feet with excitement over her discovery.

"*Shhhhh!*" scolded a bearded scholar hunched over a book nearby.

"Ooops," Will said in a loud whisper before clapping a hand over her mouth. "Sorry!"

Will sat back down and began flipping through the book eagerly. She skimmed the chapters on the Middle Ages' rough, thatched-roof architecture and on the domestic drudgery prevalent during the period. A picture showed a village square bustling with peasants in long, brown robes. Many of them stood around a crude stone well waiting patiently for water.

It's all there, Will said to herself in wonder. This is just the kind of thing I saw in Metamoor. The people who live there have these incredibly difficult lives, while Prince Phobos has all the power.

Even as a pang of sympathy stabbed her, Will felt a burst of happiness.

"Well!" she whispered. "This'll make my report loads easier. I can read some of these books. Then I'll add details from my personal experience in Metamoor. Yes!"

Will grabbed her bag off the floor and dug

inside it for a notebook and pen. She was ready to write!

Oh, she thought as her hand grazed a small, heavy gadget at the bottom of her bag. I'd better turn off my cell phone before I start working.

Will pulled out the phone. But when she reached for the OFF button, she saw that the cell's little screen was already a blank, slate gray.

Huh, Will thought. I don't remember turning this off earlier.

She flashed back on her hectic afternoon, feeling a guilty twinge as she remembered her mother's instructions on the answering machine: "I'll be late again tonight. . . . Keep your cell phone on."

Some impish side of herself must have turned the phone off just to snub her mom.

Well . . . so what? Will thought sullenly. Is it a crime to want to focus on my homework? Mom should be nothing but happy about that.

Then Will imagined her friends. They'd be getting out of school about now. Perhaps they were headed to one of their houses after school. And they weren't missing her at all.

Feeling the corners of her mouth tugging

downward, Will tossed the phone back into her bag. She hunched over her book and squinted at the crowded text.

Just focus on showing Mr. Collins what you're capable of, Will ordered herself. And forget about the phone. Nobody wants to call me, anyway.

NINE

As Irma walked down a Heatherfield sidewalk with her friends—well, all of her friends except Will—she sighed happily. She was *loving* this mission.

First of all, school was out. And Irma was *always* happiest when school was out.

Actually, it would have been even nicer if this mission had demanded that the girls *skip* school altogether. Then Irma could have totally missed that disgusting biology lesson. Was there some law that biology teachers had to gross their students out as much as humanly possible?

Like I really need to know what the inside of a worm looks like, Irma thought. Much less what a worm's innards *smell* like.

She could also have avoided that moment of humiliation between fifth and sixth periods. She'd been talking to Hay Lin when she'd noticed her friend's eyes traveling again and again to her chin.

"What?" Irma had finally demanded.

"Oh, it's nothing. . . ." Hay Lin had said slyly. "Just a mountain-sized spot on your chin is all."

"What?" Irma had screeched in panic. "Why didn't you say something earlier? Now I don't have time to go to the bathroom to deploy my emergency zit kit!"

"Just do it here," Hay Lin had offered apologetically. "I'll shield you from the prying eyes of the masses."

So Irma had crouched down against the wall while Hay Lin stood in front of her. She'd pulled a makeup bag out of her backpack and begun slathering on elements of her get-rid-of-zits-quick formula. She'd started with astringent. Then she'd applied zit cream. Next had come the cover-up stick and, finally, a light dusting of powder.

The masking method never failed Irma. And neither did Hay Lin—usually!

The thing was, Hay Lin was really skinny. There was only so much blockage her little body was capable of. Which was why, somewhere between the zit goo and the cover-up stick, Irma was noticed, by Sergei Glickov—one of Sheffield's adorable older Infielders

Peering around Hay Lin, the boy had frowned in confusion at Irma's giant zit.

"I do not understand," he had said. "What happened to you, Irma?"

Aaaiggh! Irma cringed at the memory of it. Yes, skipping school would have been better than that!

Skipping school would also have been a tremendous risk. Especially for Irma. Her dad was a police sergeant and as gruff as a bear. If Irma had ever been caught doing something really bad, like ditching school or maybe breaking and entering—another new hobby she'd taken up since becoming a Guardian—Dad's claws definitely would have come out. Irma would have been more than grounded. She'd probably have been chained to the bedpost for a month with no escape.

We're talking no sweets or superlong baths, Irma thought with a shudder. If there was anything in this world Irma loved more than hanging with her friends and flirting with boys, it was soaking in a long, hot bath. Preferably with a dish of candy or cookies teetering on the tub's edge.

Speaking of which . . . Irma returned to the present. And to the Guardians' mission. And to the reason she was so psyched about it.

The girls were *not* about to plunge through a scary and, no doubt, gross portal. They were not going to battle some lumpy blue troll or be accosted by some slithery snake.

No. They were going to eat cookies and sip tea, all the while scrutinizing their host—Mrs. Rudolph. Irma just *knew* that that lady had some tricks up her sleeve. She didn't care how sweet and plump Mrs. Rudolph was. Math teachers couldn't be trusted—especially math teachers with inner monsters.

That's actually kinda redundant, when you think about it, Irma thought with a snort of laughter.

"Shhhhh," Taranee reprimanded Irma loudly. "I'm trying to call Will."

Irma gulped back her giggle and looked around in surprise. While she'd been distracted—

what with all the cringing and daydreaming—
the four Guardians had arrived at their destina-
tion. They were standing across the street from
Mrs. Rudolph's sizable, pink house. Taranee
was in a phone booth, getting ready to call Will.

As soon as the friend made it over there,
they'd be ready to go face the math teacher.

Monster, Irma corrected herself. Or, say,
Mathster. Moncher?

Irma felt another round of giggles coming
on. She covered her mouth as Taranee dialed
Will's cell phone number.

After a long pause, Taranee shook her head
and hung up the phone.

"I got that annoying message," Taranee
reported with a worried frown. "'The subscriber
you have dialed cannot be reached. Please try
again later.'"

Irma gulped. Was Will holding a grudge
about their disagreement at lunch?

She shouldn't be, Irma thought with a
shrug. That was, like, two whole traumas ago,
by my count. But maybe Will's feeling differ-
ently.

For the first time on this mission, a trickle of
fear crawled into Irma's gut. It hadn't occurred

to her that Will might not be joining them for snacking with and spying on Mrs. Rudolph.

Something else struck Irma for the first time. What would the Guardians do if Will dropped out of W.i.t.c.h. altogether? Could they go on? How would they co—

"Did it ever cross your minds," Cornelia suddenly asked, "that Will could possibly be dispensable?"

Oh, yes, Irma thought drily. Whatever was I worried about? The minute Will steps out of the spotlight, Cornelia "Control Freak" Hale is happy to step in and take over.

She'll have to get past me first! Irma thought with a sly grin.

"Listen to me, Corny," she said, stomping over to Cornelia, who was standing on the curb looking sulky. She had purposely used a nickname that Cornelia did not like. "Without Will, I'm not going into that house."

She looked to her other friends for nods of support. But Taranee was still staring at the pay phone. And Hay Lin was completely out of it. She was gazing at Mrs. Rudolph's house across the street, a thoughtful frown darkening her usually sunny face.

Well, Irma thought, I guess I'll take Corny on alone. Not that there's anything wrong with that.

Irma loved a good battle of wits with Cornelia. That was because *Irma* always won— or, at least, got the most laughs!

Cornelia sneered at Irma.

"First of all," Cornelia told Irma, "we are perfectly capable of meeting Mrs. Rudolph by ourselves. And second—don't call me Corny!"

"What?" Irma sputtered, glancing over at Taranee and Hay Lin with a laugh. Hay Lin was still ignoring her. She was writing something on her palm with her favorite purple Magic Marker.

"It's impossible for me to stop making up nicknames for you," Irma said, turning around to face Cornelia. "That'd be like telling Hay Lin not to write on her hand anymore. You can't break lifelong habits."

"By the way," Taranee said, stepping up to Hay Lin and trying to peer over her shoulder. "What *is* she writing on her hand?"

Hay Lin finished scribbling a lengthy phrase on her palm. She cast an exaggerated look to her left. And a furtive glance to her right. Then she thrust her hand out dramatically to Taranee.

Irma left Cornelia fuming and bounded over to Taranee. Together, they squinted at Hay Lin's slightly sweaty scrawl.

"*They make us reserve . . . ?*" Irma read haltingly.

"No," Taranee said, grabbing Hay Lin's hand away from Irma. "It's something like: *Where is . . . someone?* or—"

"Hello!" Hay Lin grunted between clenched teeth. "I was *trying* to be discreet here. But since that isn't happening, I'll just go ahead and say it out loud. There is someone watching us!" Her voice sounded shaky.

"Oh!" Irma said, giving Hay Lin's palm another read. "You're right. That *is* what it says. I don't know why I didn't see that from the begin—"

Suddenly, Hay Lin's meaning actually sank in. Following her friends' alarmed gazes, Irma looked into Mrs. Rudolph's front window. The woman was indeed watching them. And smiling and waving! She motioned to the girls to come inside.

Irma gulped. Then, with her friends, she

began to walk across the street to Mrs. Rudolph's imposing, wrought-iron gate.

Will or no Will, Irma thought frantically, we're trapped. There's no getting out of our visit with Mrs. Rudolph. Oh, I'm *dreading* this mission. . . .

Five minutes later, the Guardians were perched uncomfortably in Mrs. Rudolph's formal front parlor. Taranee, Hay Lin, and Cornelia were framed by the dramatically high back of a red velvet sofa, while Irma was perched next to them in a tweed chair. Mrs. Rudolph sat in a straight-backed chair opposite Irma. On the coffee table between Mrs. Rudolph and the girls rested two platters piled high with cookies and cream puffs. There was also a full tea service, with cream-and-gold cups and saucers.

Gee, Irma thought, fingering the lacy doily on the arm of her chair. Metamoorian monsters sure have fussy taste. Right down to their dainty china and fancy treats.

She was just reaching for her little cup when it began floating in the air!

All five of the cups, along with their saucers,

began levitating off the coffee table! They were quickly followed by the steaming teapot. All on its own, the pot neatly poured jasmine-scented tea into every cup. Next, a set of silver tongs drifted around, depositing lunps of sugar into the cups. It plunked two into Irma's before the cup floated into her stunned hands.

"I had a feeling you liked your tea sweet," Mrs. Rudolph said to Irma with a smile. "Do you take milk, too?"

Irma merely shook her head dumbly. Meanwhile, Cornelia gaped at their serene-looking host.

"I guess it's safe to say you have powers, Mrs. Rudolph," she gasped. She ducked as the teapot swooped just a bit too close to her button nose.

"Making cups and spoons levitate isn't a power," Mrs. Rudolph scoffed. "I call it . . . a useful gift. All my fellow Metamoorians have magical capabilities. Of course," she added, catching her own cup and saucer deftly and inhaling her tea's fragrance. "Our magic is nothing compared to yours."

Irma took a sip of tea as the girls digested that sobering fact. Then she spoke up: "Why did you invite us here? Do you have anything to tell us?"

"The last time we met," Mrs. Rudolph recalled, "I was hiding in Metamoor's underground. Wandering about those dark places, I had a chance to meet many refugees—rebels who hate Phobos."

Irma's eyes widened. Rebels living underground? Cooool!

"Some of the most resentful and well-trained rebels have presented themselves to Vathek," Mrs. Rudolph continued.

Vathek! Irma thought in alarm. That big, blue guy?

Soon after the girls had discovered they were Guardians, Vathek had provided Irma's rude introduction to the oh-so-unattractive baddies of Metamoor.

Some welcoming committee, Irma thought. Vathek snatched me and Hay Lin up in his huge, meaty paws and got ready to throw us into a pit that led straight to the earth's core! If Will hadn't saved us, we'd have been sunk.

Feeling a pang for her missing friend, Irma returned her attention to Mrs. Rudolph.

"Vathek, as you know, is Cedric's servant," Mrs. Rudolph explained. "He's told the rebels that he's left his master, and he's offering to put his knowledge at their service. Of course, he's a pretty unreliable source!"

"But . . . what if it's the truth?" Hay Lin wondered aloud.

Mrs. Rudolph pursed her lips and paused.

Ah, a lapse in the conversation, Irma thought. An excellent opportunity to snag a cookie or three. Hmmm, I'll take this pink one with chocolate filling. Oooh, and one of those shortbreads. . . .

As Irma began munching happily, Mrs. Rudolph planted her cup on the coffee table. She looked hard at the trio on the love seat.

"Let's be honest, girls," she declared. "Do you trust me?"

"Of course . . ." Taranee said, with a slight tremor in her voice.

"Sure . . ." Hay Lin said, tentatively.

"Oh . . . certainly," Cornelia piped up with a big, fake smile on her face.

"Uh-huh," Mrs. Rudolph said drily. "Then why haven't you touched the tea and cookies? Do you think they're poisoned?"

Irma stopped in mid-bite.

She painfully swallowed her mouthful of cookie.

Then she glanced over at her friends. Each of them was cradling a brimming cup of tea. And their laps? They were completely crumbless.

Boycotting the goodies, Irma thought, cringing. Smart move. I wish I'd thought of that. But since it's obviously too late . . .

"Uh . . ." Irma spoke up with wide eyes. "They *aren't* poisoned, are they?"

A voice jangled in Irma's head. But it wasn't Mrs. Rudolph's answer.

Uh-oh, Irma thought in a panic. Is this the poison taking effect? Am I hearing the voices of angels?

Tell me, Irma! Weren't you the one who was afraid of Mrs. Rudolph?

Oh. That was no angel. That was just Taranee, speaking to Irma via telepathy.

Irma did a quick poison scan. She wiggled her fingers. No numbness. She blinked her eyes. Her vision was totally nonblurry. She waggled her tongue. No swellage there!

She was A-OK!

So, now, she could answer Taranee with her own thoughts.

Well, yeah, she said sheepishly. *But these cookies are clearly harmless.*

"Yes, they are, in fact," Mrs. Rudolph said, grabbing the cookie plate off the coffee table and passing it to Taranee. "Why don't you try a coconut one, dear? They're delicious!"

"What?" Taranee gasped. "You can read our thoughts?"

Again, Mrs. Rudolph merely flashed a cryptic smile.

Suddenly, Taranee gasped and slapped her forehead.

"But this morning, in math class . . ."

Mrs. Rudolph waved Taranee's horror away.

"Let's talk about more serious matters," she said. "Now, you can understand how hard it is to trust Vathek. . . ."

Irma and her friends nodded.

"Well, Vathek has convinced a group of desperate rebels to try to invade earth," Mrs. Rudolph said somberly. "Tonight!"

"When, exactly?" Hay Lin gasped.

"He was going to try to recruit other rebels to join them," Mrs. Rudolph said, rising from her chair. "But the invasion is scheduled for seven P.M."

Irma looked at the grandfather clock in the parlor's corner.

"Oh, no!" she cried. "It's already five!"

Cornelia put her teacup down and jumped to her feet.

"Do you know which of the portals they'll be coming through?" she asked Mrs. Rudolph.

"No, unfortunately," Mrs. Rudolph said. "I hoped you could tell *me* that."

Hay Lin popped out of her seat as well and dashed into the foyer. When she returned, she was clutching her backpack. She flipped open the top flap and pulled out a yellowed scroll of parchment. Irma recognized the rolled document immediately. It was the beautiful, highly detailed map of Heatherfield that Hay Lin's grandmother had passed on to Hay Lin before she died. When a particular portal was gearing up for action, it sometimes showed up as a glowing red light on the map.

"Here's the map of the portals," Hay Lin announced. "But without the Heart of Candracar . . ."

"That's right," Irma realized with regret.

"The portals only glow when Will releases the Heart over the map."

Irma remembered the first time she'd witnessed that little miracle. Will had held her tightly clenched fist over the map and closed her eyes. Whorls of pink magic had seeped through Will's fingers and swirled around her body like a wonderful, cotton-candy cloak. Will's red hair had stood on end. Finally, Will had unclenched her fist with a happy gasp. Hovering over her palm in a burst of pink light had been a glass orb, cradled in an asymmetrical silver clasp. It was the Heart of Candracar.

And it was also an excellent homing device. The orb would float out of Will's reach and skim over the map until it came to a decisive rest over, say, the shell cave on the beach or Cedric's bookstore. And sure enough, when the Guardians investigated, they had discovered portals in those places.

There's no way to find them otherwise, Irma thought in despair.

Mrs. Rudolph clearly wasn't so sure of this. Neither, of course, was Cornelia. As Mrs. Rudolph led the girls into her dining room, then spread the map out on her long, mahogany table, Cornelia stared at the page defiantly.

"Let's figure this out by deduction," Mrs. Rudolph proposed. "Where in Heatherfield did you encounter Cedric?"

"In the gym," Irma said, shuddering as she once again recalled her run-in with Vathek. After Will had saved them from the blue thug, the girls had discovered that the snaky Cedric had been lurking in the shadows. He'd been the one who'd ordered Vathek to harm them.

"But, when we saw him there," Irma added, "we closed that portal after we broke free of Vathek."

"Wait!" Taranee exclaimed suddenly. "The bookshop! After all, Cedric owned it."

"Yes," Mrs. Rudolph agreed. "It's the perfect place for the rebels to make their passage."

Cornelia pumped her fist in the air.

"So, let's go," she declared to her friends. "There's no time to lose!"

"Just a moment, Cornelia," Irma said. She walked around the dining room table to stand between Taranee and Hay Lin. She wanted to take on their rebellious blonde as part of a united front.

"To face an entire army," she declared, "we need Will. You *know* this."

This time, Taranee was on her side.

"I agree with Irma," she said. "We've got to track Will down."

Hay Lin nodded vigorously.

Irma gazed at Cornelia in triumph. As she'd said—she always won their skirmishes.

And as usual, Cornelia wasn't exactly gracious in her defeat. She was rather annoyed, but nodded reluctantly.

"All right," she sighed. "Let's split up and find her. But with or without Will, we meet up in front of Cedric's bookstore at six-thirty tonight. That will give us just enough time to face . . . the rebels!"

TEN

Will rode her bike home from the library on a cloud of triumph. Her report rocked! Her quick research on the politics of the Middle Ages, as well as all of the sights, smells, and gloomy feelings she'd absorbed during her visits to Metamoor—all were in there. In thirty heavy pages, to be exact!

Will knew she should worry more about the quality of her writing than the quantity, but, hey, she'd never written a thirty-page report before. She felt like a supergirl.

Of course, Will thought with a giggle, maybe that's my magical powers talking.

As she turned in to the parking lot of her building, though, Will's smile faded.

Uh-oh, she thought. Mom's car is

here. She must have gotten home early! By now, I bet Mr. Collins has had time to leave her a voice mail about my out-of-school adventure today.

Will clamped her little rubber-frog key chain between her teeth as she negotiated her bike in to the rack in front of her building. She headed for the front door. She'd almost reached it when she saw something that stopped her in her tracks.

Was it a blue, lumpish creature, ready to pound her?

Cedric the snake-man? Phobos the pillager?

No. It was a green hatchback with a pinecone-shaped air freshener dangling from the rearview mirror.

Okay, Will thought, feeling dread settle into her stomach like sour milk. I guess it's a pretty safe bet that Mr. Collins has ratted me out to Mom. That's his car! He's here!

With a heavy sigh, Will trudged into the building. She ignored the open elevator doors and took the stairs. She didn't want to arrive home any sooner than she had to.

Reaching her floor, Will walked down the hall reluctantly. She eyed her apartment door, a wary expression on her face.

Behind that door lurked . . . Mr. Collins.

Ugh, Will thought, jangling her key chain in agitation. Who knows what kind of lies he's told my mother about me?

She was just about to turn her key in the lock when, suddenly, she heard those very lies coming through the door. Well, she heard Mr. Collins's voice, anyway. And then she heard her own name!

He *is* talking about me, Will fumed silently. That totally gives me the right to eavesdrop, for, say . . . thirty seconds.

Will pressed her ear to the keyhole and tried to home in on Mr. Collins's voice. It sounded murky through the thick, metal door. But she could just make out what he was saying.

"Will's a smart girl," Mr. Collins declared. "Very sensitive and intelligent."

Will paused. Was Mr. Collins actually . . . defending her? After the way he'd bullied her in class today? He must have been buttering up her mom, she thought.

And now, Mom was answering. Her stern voice sounded distinctly unmoved.

"Don't dissuade me, Dean," she insisted. "I

have to punish her. She skipped school!"

"Come on, Susan," Mr. Collins cajoled. "Will doesn't act impulsively. She must have had a good reason."

"Well . . ." Mom was hesitating. Will could just picture her mother's face, set in a stubborn frown, her arms crossed over her chest.

". . . Will could have at least left her cell phone on," Mom complained.

That's it, Mom, Will thought, rolling her eyes. If at first you don't find something legit to pin on me, try, try again!

"What worries me," Mom continued, "is not knowing where she is."

I'll take care of that, Will thought darkly. She suddenly twisted her key in the lock. The door opened with a loud, echoing *clack*. Will sidled through the door with her eyes downcast. One quick glance confirmed Will's fears. Her mother was pacing the length of the loft with her arms folded. Mr. Collins sat on the edge of one of the red chairs, a troubled look on his face.

At Will's entrance, her mom stopped pacing. She gave her daughter a withering look, then gazed over at Mr. Collins.

"You talk to her, Dean," she said. "I don't even know how to react right now."

But before Mr. Collins could say anything, Will herself spoke up.

"Forgive me, Mother," she said with heavy formality. "There really isn't much to say."

No, Will thought angrily. I'll let my *work* speak for me.

Reaching into her bag, Will pulled out the heavy sheaf of papers that constituted her report. Then she marched over to Mr. Collins and shoved the report into his hands.

Without glancing at her mother, Will turned on her heel and headed straight back toward the door.

"I'll be going to the swimming pool, now," she declared. "See you."

Slam!

Will found herself standing outside the loft door, breathing hard.

"Whew!" she whispered incredulously. "I did it! I totally stuck it to my mom! I'm surprised she didn't follow me. She can be such a hothead."

Will was just getting ready to rush down the hall when she heard Mr. Collins's voice echoing through the door once again. Pressing her ear to the door, she heard him say, "It's a report on the life of people living in the Middle Ages. About thirty pages!"

Let's hear it for quantity, Will cheered inwardly. She couldn't help but feel a zing of pride at how impressed Mr. Collins sounded.

"What is this about?" Will heard her mom asking.

"I don't know," Mr. Collins replied. "But it looks excellent!"

He doesn't know? Will thought indignantly. I guess it's easy for him to forget about assignments he hands out without a thought. *He* doesn't have to spend hours in a creepy library completing them.

Her mom was speaking again.

"Excellent," she repeated drily. "Well, that makes sense. Will's such a hothead, after all."

Hothead! Will thought. Me! Oh, that's just perfect. She should look in the mirro—

"Okay, then," Mr. Collins said behind the door, interrupting Will's silent rant. "She reminds me of someone I know."

Will clapped a surprised hand over her mouth.

That's the first time Mr. Collins and I have ever agreed on anything, she thought grimly. But that doesn't mean I like him, or anything.

With a curt nod to no one, Will strode to the elevator. As she stepped into the closet-sized elevator, she glanced back at her apartment door. She pictured her mother, a few hours from now, pacing the floor and wondering where she'd gone.

Well . . . maybe I've pushed things far enough, Will admitted to herself. I'll just turn on my cell phone. It's not *really* for Mom's benefit. After all, I might want to make a call. . . .

As she pushed the elevator's lobby button, Will fished around in her messy gym bag for her cell phone. But when she pulled it out and hit the ON button, she was shocked to see that the screen remained gray and blank.

It's dead? Will thought. I charged the battery last night. It should have hours left in it.

Suddenly, Will remembered her favorite power—her ability to talk to electronic appliances! She'd had a running dialogue going with her refrigerator, TV, computer, and printer for a while, now. Why not try it with her cell phone? She'd just *ask* it what happened.

"Uh, hello? Cell?" Will said to her phone.

Sure enough, the gadget's screen went neon green, and a little battery symbol—indicating that the battery was drained—popped up. Then a nasal voice that reminded Will of the phone operators in old movies spoke.

"What do you want? What do you want?" the phone demanded.

Will grinned.

"Enough with the echo," she admonished the phone. "This isn't three-way calling!"

"Only because I'm outdated," the phone groused. "Another generation younger and I could have had a built-in camera."

Will laughed, just as the elevator doors opened. She sauntered into the lobby and was about to ask her question when the phone came on again.

"And anyway," it said. "You should have more respect for me. Am I not your substitute mother, after all?"

"C'mon," Will said cajolingly. She'd learned that all her appliances responded best to a placating tone. "Don't get all ruffled. Just tell me why your battery's dead, please."

"Ask your friend," the cell phone snapped

back at her in irritation. "*She* was the one who switched me off."

"Wait a minute," Will said. "What friend are you talking about?"

The cell phone uttered a name.

And Will felt her head begin to spin.

"What?" she squeaked. "But . . . that's impossible!"

Yeah, like monsters and alternate universes and teenagers with wings are impossible, Will thought. Just like the idea that I can trust *any-one* is impossible.

Will stumbled outside. Her vision was blurred by tears of hurt; her head was buzzing with incredulity.

All she wanted to do was slump down onto the curb, bury her face in her arms, and sob away all the rotten revelations of the last few hours.

But instead . . . she got mad.

A short bike ride later, at precisely six P.M., Will stalked into the Sheffield swimming center. It was eerily quiet but for the gentle *thwup-thwup-thwup* of water licking the sides of the pool. All the student swimmers seemed to have gone home.

Normally, Will would have found the empty body of blue water irresistible. She would have stripped down immediately to her bathing suit and dived in for a round of blissfully unob-structed laps.

But this evening, she barely saw the water. She had eyes only for the slender woman with the long, blond ponytail returning a life pre-server and kickboard to the bin of accessories at the pool's far end.

"Vera!" Will barked. She planted her feet at the edge of the deep end and watched Vera straighten up and turn around. The coach walked to the edge of the shallow end, directly opposite Will. Fifty meters of chlorine-scented water separated them, but the building's curved ceiling carried their voices easily.

"Are you busy?" Will asked her coach.

"No, Will," Vera replied with a smile. "In fact, I was just looking for you. Why aren't you wearing your swimsuit yet?"

"Let me ask *you* a question," Will coun-tered. "Why isn't anybody here?"

"I've convinced the pool directors to give you some free time," Vera replied. "At least three hours' worth."

"All for me?" Will said skeptically. Her hands tightened into fists. That was when she realized that she was still clutching her cell phone in her left hand. She hadn't even realized she'd been holding on to it on the bike ride over.

Thinking about the dishonest act that had caused her phone to end up without batteries, Will turned sly herself.

"You have a lot of power, don't you, Vera?" she asked.

"Well, I'm only a trainer," Vera responded chirpily. "But they listen to me and—"

"Perhaps my question wasn't clear enough," Will interrupted. "What I meant was, What *spell* did you use to convince the directors to give us the pool?"

"I don't understand," Vera said, blinking innocently.

Will thrust her cell phone toward Vera.

"You have magical abilities!" Will announced boldly. "A little bird—my cell phone—told me!"

Vera looked very far away in the vast swimming center. But even from this distance, Will could see the woman's face change. It went from sweet to stony in under a second.

Vera's shoulders stiffened beneath her pink sweatshirt.

Her eyes changed most of all. They became cold and gray.

"Well," Vera said drily. "You've finally figured it out. You don't know how hard that acting job was for me."

The cold flicker in Vera's eyes had been a blip compared to the shape-shifting the swimming coach was undergoing now! Her golden mane separated into two long, yellow plaits of a dull, strawlike color.

Her body grew shorter and more angular.

Her face melted for a moment into a putty-like, nondescript mass—a blank oval on top of a stick figure.

But in the next moment, it began to regain shape. Where Vera's pert nose and plush lips had been, new features began to form—the wan, wide eyes and pointy chin of . . .

"Elyon!" Will gasped.

ELEVEN

Irma poked her head through the doors of the Sheffield swimming center and took a deep breath.

Ahhhh, she thought. A big pool of chlorinated blue stuff. Now, that's what I like to smell.

And Will Vandom! Irma thought, spotting Will standing at one end of the pool. That's what I like to *see*! I found her! Which means, not only can she lead us in battle against the rebels, but I can also totally rub my triumph in Cornelia's face!

Irma was opening her mouth to call out to her friend when something made her stop. It was Will's posture: her feet were planted as if she were about to jump out of a starting gate. Her fists were clenched. And her jaw jutted forward in rage. She looked mad!

Clearly, something was going down!

Irma followed Will's gaze to the other end of the pool. Will was confronting that new swim coach, Vera!

That's strange, Irma thought. Will thinks Vera is the best coach. At least, that's how she's been talking about her ever since Vera arrived at Sheffield. But now, she looks ready for a catfight. Maybe they're having a disagreement over practice time or relay teams or something like that. Whatever it is, it's gonna have to wait. Metamoorian battle trumps catfight with a teacher any day.

Irma glanced at the alluring water one more time as she got ready to summon Will.

But then, something *else* made her stop.

The water just beyond Vera's toes was swirling! And wafting out of that sudden whirlpool were silvery wisps of magic!

Was Vera from Metamoor, too?

Who next? Irma thought in despair. My mailman? The clerk at the Quickie Mart on the corner?

Irma dragged her eyes away from the

swirling water to glance at Vera's face. Had it mutated into a fleshy mask of scales and horns, like Mrs. Rudolph's? Perhaps Vera had turned blue and lumpy. Or maybe she looked like . . .

Elyon! Irma gasped. While Irma had been transfixed by the magic in the water, Vera had changed into the Guardians' pigtailed nemesis.

And Will was *not* happy about it.

"How were you able to change your appearance?" she demanded of Elyon.

"Cedric is a good teacher," Elyon replied with a mischievous grin. "Did you finish the report he asked you to do?"

"What?" Will barked loudly. "He . . . was Mr. Collins?"

"Oh, yes," Elyon laughed. "You can't trust anybody. Now, just stay where you are. . . ."

As Will braced herself for a fight, Irma felt a stab of guilt. Mr. Collins *had* been an impostor! That was why Will had had that dizzy spell when she'd walked by his desk. Irma and the others should have believed her!

But why hadn't Will grown faint around Vera if Vera had actually been Elyon?

It must be because Elyon was Will's—and our—friend, Irma thought with an angry grimace.

As Irma brooded, she saw something out of the corner of her eye. Elyon was motioning toward the water. And it was responding like an obedient dog. Make that an obedient . . . sea serpent! The water was arranging itself into a long snake that was slowly undulating out of the water.

Irma glanced quickly at Will.

She felt the blood drain from her face.

Will hadn't even noticed the water snake! She had been too busy staring malevolently at Elyon's eyes.

"Just tell me one thing," she demanded of Elyon. "Why?"

"I don't know everything," Elyon hurled back. She dropped her hands to her sides sulkily and added, "It's Cedric's plan. And I trust him. My only mission was to hold you back, fair and square. But since you have now discovered me . . ."

Elyon's eyes narrowed and she lifted her hands again.

". . . I'll have to resort to *not*-so-fair means," she said, by way of finishing.

Cupping her palms and pointing her hands upward, Elyon motioned toward the water, drawing it up, up, up out of the pool.

And making it bigger, bigger, bigger!

There was no way Will could miss the water snake now! It was as tall as a rearing dragon, and just as vicious!

"Yah!" Elyon exhorted the snake, throwing her arms into the air.

Irma spotted Will through the serpent's watery coils. Will stared at the writhing creature in disbelief. By that point, it had begun to undulate all over the pool. While its long body bucked toward the ceiling and came dangerously close to the windows, its head made its way straight toward Will!

And how was Will reacting? In a way *only* another Guardian could have predicted. Instead of screaming or running or flailing at the snake with her fists, Will clenched her right hand in front of her, then closed her eyes. Wisps of pink magic began to break through from between her fingers.

She's summoning the Heart of Candracar, Irma realized. She's going to transform herself into a winged superhero and totally kick that snake's butt! If, uh, snakes have butts, that is. Hmmm, maybe I *should* start paying closer attention in bio—oh, *no!*

While Will had been summoning her magical alter ego and Irma was musing about snakes' bodies, the water serpent had simply taken action! It snatched Will up in its watery coils. Now it flung her back and forth in the air as if she was nothing more than a toy.

"*Aaaaagh!*" Will screamed down at Elyon. "Get this thing off me!"

Elyon responded by grinning—and shaking her head.

That's it, Irma thought, rolling up her sleeves. Time to make my entrance.

Stepping over to the edge of the pool, Irma yelled, "Elyon can't hear you, Will. Perhaps she's got water in her ears!"

"Irma?" Elyon called with a scowl.

Irma merely smirked at her foe. Then she raised her own arms and summoned up her magic. Immediately, blue swirls began emanating from her fingertips.

"What do you know?" she quipped to Elyon. "I have the power of water! Which means, it's time to return our water snake to its cage!"

Irma steeled her shoulders for a fight and

pointed at the slimy serpent.

"Enough!" Irma yelled. "Put her down!"

Then she gasped. It had worked! The water snake was obeying her orders!

But as the snake's topmost coil—the one in which Will was ensnared—began hurtling downward, Irma slapped her forehead in frustration.

"I should have told it to put Will down *gently*," she cried in chagrin.

"*Whooo-AAAAAHHHHH!*" Will screeched. Now that the snake had released her, she was skimming down its coils as if she were riding a death-defying waterslide!

The snake collapsed into its former state—a mere mass of water. And Will was enfolded in the cascade! A bubble bounced her to the right. A swirl batted her to the left.

Finally, she plunged into the pool, shrieking all the way. She landed with a *thwack* and a gargantuan splash.

Irma threw her hands over her head and cringed.

"Thank goodness Will is a good swimmer," she whispered to herself fearfully. "At least, I think she is!"

As the snake disappeared entirely, Irma scanned the pool's choppy surface for her friend.

There she was! Will's head had just popped out of the water, gasping for breath. She began to swim energetically toward Irma.

Okay, Irma thought, Will's done her job—she's survived. Now it's time for me to do mine—trouncing Elyon!

"We're down to a face-off," Irma declared to Elyon, who still stood on the opposite side of the pool, looking smug. "Just you and me, Elyon!"

"Don't count on it, Irma," Elyon spat. New silvery swirls began to undulate around her like a cloak of clouds. "But don't worry. We'll see each other soon."

Elyon started to grow transparent! A moment later, she evaporated into thin air.

"She's disappeared!" Irma cried in despair.

Will pulled herself over to the swimming-pool wall and turned around. She gazed at the empty spot where Elyon had stood only a second ago.

"She must have teletransported herself," Will gasped. She was still coughing up mouthfuls of water after her ordeal with the snake.

"Here," Irma said, reaching down to help Will out of the pool.

Will grabbed her hand and hauled herself out of the water.

"I had no idea Elyon could be that powerful," Will breathed, slumping at the pool's edge. "Even if Cedric *is* her mentor."

Irma could only nod. It seemed as though Elyon was getting more powerful with every visitation! And more scary!

While Irma quietly freaked, Will caught her breath and began squeezing the moisture out of her hair. Then she flashed Irma a grateful look.

"Thanks for the save," she said. "Even if that dive was, uh, less than fun. How did you guess that I was here?"

Irma shrugged.

"We have this in common," she said, gesturing at the pool. "This is your favorite place, and it's also the most obvious place for *me* to look for you!"

Will's next question was unspoken, but Irma could see it in her still-hurt brown eyes: And why were you looking for me, Irma? To apologize? To eat crow? Or to give me more bad news about our war with the Metamoorian baddies?

Unfortunately, the answer was number three.

Irma bit her lip and said, "We've got to start walking, now! We've got a long way to go and not much time. So hurry up, and I'll explain everything on the road."

TWELVE

Cornelia paced back and forth in front of Cedric's bookshop. She looked at her watch for about the twelfth time in three minutes.

The first time she'd looked, it had been six-twenty-seven.

Which meant it was now six-thirty—the time Cornelia had insisted all the Guardians gather.

But only she, Hay Lin, and Taranee were there.

"Well," Cornelia said, dragging her gaze away from her watch face to regard her friends. They were huddled together on a bus stop bench on the sidewalk. They looked pale and worried. "We have no choice but to get started. There's no sign of the others."

"Great," Hay Lin sighed. "Now it's not just Will who's missing. Irma's gone, too! What should we do, Cornelia?"

Cornelia froze. Hay Lin was gazing at her with a mixture of fear, admiration, and urgent need. It was a look that lately had been reserved solely for Will—the group's leader.

Now that Hay Lin was giving *her* that look, Cornelia had to admit it to herself—it didn't feel as great as she'd expected it to.

"I don't know what we should do," she moaned, putting a hand to her forehead. "Leave me alone for a minute. I've got to think."

Willing her mind to kick into gear only made it go rebelliously blank. Cornelia frowned in frustration.

Why can't decisions, she thought, just fall from the sky?

Claannnnggggg!

Well what do you know?—something had just fallen from the sky!

Cornelia jumped as that something crashed into a lamppost only a couple of feet away from her. Then it hurtled to the sidewalk, landing with a sickening crunch.

Cornelia gaped at the object as it shuddered to a halt. It was . . . a bicycle! A red bicycle with a yellow seat. It looked familiar. . . .

Cornelia glanced up at the top of the lamppost. Sure enough, the bike's owner—Will—was clinging to the pillar with all four limbs. She was breathing hard and hanging on tightly with all of her strength.

Just below her, already beginning to grin and giggle, was Irma.

"Will! Irma!" Cornelia shrieked. Hay Lin and Taranee had jumped to their feet and run over to join her. "How did you get here?"

"Well . . ." Irma said, with a sheepish shrug. "Witches use brooms to fly. I thought we'd use a bike! The landing was a toughie, though!"

Will merely added, *"Aaaaccchooo!"*

"Will is all wet," Irma added, shinnying down the lamppost and hopping over to the other Guardians. Slowly, Will slid down the lamppost after her.

"During the flight over here," Irma explained, "she definitely—"

"—Caught a cold," Will cried, with an unhappy sniff.

Cornelia gaped at Will. And then she

started to laugh! She didn't know if it was relief at having their leader back in their midst or amusement at the thought of Irma and Will careening through the skies on a red bike. Whatever it was, it felt good!

Taranee and Hay Lin quickly joined in. Meanwhile, Irma said to Will guiltily, "The end justifies the means."

Will nodded ruefully.

Which made Cornelia realize just what a good team member Will was. She was ready to do her duty—and battle at her friend's side—no matter what kind of ache she was still feeling after the whole lunch hour run-in.

If that didn't make Will a leader of their haphazard little family, Cornelia didn't know what did. And it was time to swallow her pride and say so to Will.

She stepped forward, swallowing hard, and put a hand on Will's shoulder.

"Will," she said apologetically. "I—"

"Let's have our talk after this," Will said quickly. But she did give Cornelia an understanding, forgiving look. "And while we're at it, I think we have to forgo an elaborate plan of action. There's no time. We simply have to trust our powers." She looked at them knowingly.

Will closed her eyes. Cornelia followed suit. She knew what was coming. Will's body would contort itself as magic surged through her muscles, her veins, even her heart! And when she opened her palm, another heart would be floating above it—the Heart of Candracar.

"Cornelia!" Will called out. "Earth!"

Cornelia's eyes flew open in time to see Will send a teardrop of concentrated green magic from the Heart of Candracar straight toward her. The droplet swirled around Cornelia as she felt its power suffuse her own veins and every muscle.

Cornelia's body contracted. She felt her arms and legs growing longer and stronger. Her hair was growing, too. And she knew her face was becoming more angular, more grown-up and more knowing. Best of all, her green skirt and practical brown jacket were falling away, to be replaced by a sweeping purple skirt, a midriff-baring, off-the-shoulder top, and a pair of fluttering, iridescent wings.

As Cornelia was transformed, Will sent a watery, blue teardrop to Irma, a fiery one to Taranee, and a silver bundle of air to Hay Lin.

Then she let the Heart's pink energy envelop her own body.

Within seconds, the girls had become Guardians—smart, beautiful, and powerful.

Emphasis on the powerful, Cornelia thought. Will had just stepped up to the bookshop's door—which mostly consisted of a cloudy glass window. After trying the antique brass doorknob and finding the door locked, she'd tapped the glass with her fist. The single blow had shattered the window, sending shards flying.

"What an entrance!" Hay Lin said as the Guardians stepped through the window into the dark and dusty bookstore. "Are you sure we should just barge in like this?"

"Hey," Will said with a grin. "The mat on the front step says 'Welcome,' doesn't it?"

"As do I," said a thin, but sinister, voice in the back of the store. It was a voice Cornelia knew well.

Elyon!

En masse, the Guardians stumbled farther into the shop, peering back into the gloom. Cornelia saw a flash of blond hair. There she was! Elyon was peeking through the back office door at the Guardians, grinning at them mischievously.

"Welcome," Elyon said again, sarcastically. "If you're looking for a particular book, just follow me to the back."

Then she disappeared.

"Elyon!" Cornelia huffed to her friends in frustration. "What does she have do with all this?"

"I'll explain after," Will said breathlessly. "Now we have to follow her."

Cornelia didn't have time to be annoyed that Will was in the know while she was in the dark. They had to find Elyon! The girls plunged through the office door into the back.

Well, at least now we're *all* in the dark, Cornelia thought drily.

Until, of course, Taranee created a fireball in the palm of her hand and sent it bobbling toward the ceiling. Now the girls could see, but it didn't do them much good. All they encountered was a large room, crowded with looming bookshelves. The very tall shelves were arranged tightly, to create narrow aisles. But near the door, where the girls were standing, was a clearing of sorts. It was a square space about the size of a small apartment—with bookshelves for walls. As far as the eye could see, there were nothing but books and . . .

Wait a minute, Cornelia thought as she glanced into one corner. Was that Elyon?

She'd thought she'd seen a flash of her old friend's long, blue dress.

But before Cornelia could tell the others about the sighting, Irma cried out, "She just disappeared behind those shelves!"

Cornelia glanced at Irma. She was pointing at the opposite side of the room entirely!

"No," Hay Lin yelled, pointing to yet another corner. "She's over there."

"That's not possible," Irma insisted. "I just saw her on the other side!"

Sighing in frustration, Cornelia spun around in a circle. Elyon was playing games with them agai—

Hey! This time Cornelia *knew* she wasn't imagining it. Elyon was gazing at her from between two tall bookshelves.

"Elyon!" she cried.

But, of course, Elyon turned on her heel and disappeared into the dark corridor.

"Wait!" Cornelia screamed, taking a few steps forward. "It's Cornelia!"

"That's not your friend anymore," Irma said, reminding Cornelia. "She's the opposite of that. And we've got to stop her!"

Cornelia felt a wave of sadness wash over her. She knew Irma was right. Elyon had *once* been her best friend, the keeper of all of Cornelia's secrets, and number one on her cell phone's speed dial. But that always smiling, boy-crazy girl seemed to have disappeared.

"If I could just speak to her," Cornelia said wistfully. "For a moment!"

"Wait," Will cut in. "Did you see where she went?"

Together, the girls pressed forward and ducked into the aisle where they'd last spotted Elyon. Taranee beckoned her fireball and the light source bobbled after them.

The aisle went only a short distance before it turned a corner to the right. Then it veered sharply to the left.

And then it split in two!

"She's led us into a trap," Will said in shock. "Or she wants to mislead us."

"Or . . ." Irma quavered, looking around.

"Um, guys? Do you have the same nasty feeling that I do? That this maze of a bookshop has become . . . an actual labyrinth?"

Cornelia darted forward to peer down both sides of the divided corridor. One row of bookshelves began to curve in a seemingly endless coil. The other turned a corner. Irma was right! They were trapped inside with no way out!

"I hope this is a magic trick," Irma observed, looking up at the sky-high furniture boxing them in. "If not, just imagine how many customers get lost in this bookshop every day!"

Unngggh. Will clutched her head and let out a woozy moan.

Cornelia looked at her in alarm. Taranee grabbed Will's shoulders before she could faint.

"Is everything all right, Will?" Taranee asked in alarm.

"I'm okay," Will said, a moment later. She blinked the haziness from her eyes and shook away her dizziness. "It's my usual faint feeling. The invasion clearly has begun. I can feel it!" She steeled herself. It looked as though her strength had returned quickly this time. And her bravery wasn't too shabby, either. She set off down the left fork and motioned to her friends.

"Follow me," she said. "I'll try to always turn east among these shelves, so we don't get too lost. Hopefully, my faintness will lead us to its source!"

Will's hope paid off too quickly. The Guardians had only to round a corner before they ran into a crowd of scaly Metamoorians, clambering through a portal. The roiling tunnel of silver magic and otherworldly vapor had erupted right in the middle of the maze's wide aisle. It hovered in the air, swirling and growling like a wild beast.

Speaking of beasts, the rebels emerging from the portal looked like Metamoor's most absolutely scruffy, warty inhabitants. Their long, medieval robes were tattered and dirty. Their scaly hands were gnarled. Their beady, red eyes looked uniformly hungry. And angry!

And no pair of eyes was more peeved than that of the big, blue thug Vathek. When the Guardians rounded the corner, he had been at the head of the group of rebels, urging them to hurry out of the bookstore.

But, of course, the moment Cornelia and her friends made their appearance, Vathek changed his mind.

"The Guardians!" he bellowed to his motley crew. "Get them!"

Roaring with aggression, the rebels whipped swords from their belts. Some of the weapons had blades of steel. Others were tipped by crackling, lightninglike energy, which, frankly, looked a lot more sinister than steel.

"Didn't I say I wished this was a magic trick?" Irma cried. "Why couldn't I keep my big mouth shut?"

"Well, we've got some magic of our own, don't we?" Hay Lin said. "I think I'll send mine by *air* mail!"

Hay Lin levitated into the air and thrust her hands out at the invaders. A magic-tinged gust of wind hit a cluster of the Metamoorians smack in their stomachs. With a collective roar, they stumbled backward, shielding their eyes against the tremendous gust.

Cornelia balled up her own fists, readying her magic to shake the rebels. But before she had a chance to crack open the floor or make the bookshelves collapse, Taranee gathered an armful of fire. She stopped herself, however, before she hurled it at the baddies.

"Wait—there are tons of books here," she

cried. "I don't want to risk burning down the whole building!"

"Irma can wash away the fire," Will declared.

"How?" Irma asked. "I have power over water, but there are no fire hydrants here! I can't just wring the stuff out of the air!"

"Okay!" Will said, confidently changing her plan. "Forget the creatures. Let's concentrate on the portal. We have to close it at all costs."

Nodding in agreement, Cornelia joined forces with her friend. She focused on the portal, trying at the same time to keep the rebels in her peripheral vision. She didn't want any rude interruptions in the middle of performing a magic exploit!

In a few seconds, though, she realized something.

Not only were the rebels not interrupting the Guardians—they were ignoring them completely! Instead, they were all looking at . . .

Cornelia followed the monsters' gaze.

. . . Cedric! He was standing at the end of the aisle in a flowing purple coat. His pinched, beautiful face was as smug as ever. He stared down the battling rebels and the Guardians.

Cornelia gasped.

So *that* was why Elyon was here. She was reporting to Cedric. And Cedric is . . .

"A servant of Phobos!" cried one of the monsters in a raspy howl. He pointed at Cedric in rage.

Yup, Cornelia thought. Which pretty much makes us *all* enemies here. This is getting confusing!

But not for the rebels. Suddenly, they couldn't have cared less about the Guardians.

"Catch him!" a big, floppy-eared, blue thug yelled.

Irma—who had been halfway through walloping Vathek—paused in the midst of her fisticuffs.

"What are they doing?" she demanded. "They're against Cedric?"

"Not against him," Vathek growled. "But what he represents—years of lies. Of poverty. Of *suffering*!"

A beast with a fringe of plantlike, green hair cascading from his chin ran up to Cedric. Before the evil lord could raise his slender hands in protest—or mutate into a sinister snake, for that matter—the monster had grabbed Cedric's long, blond locks. Yanking the man's head back sharply, the rebel forced him to his knees.

"Let go of me," Cedric ordered imperiously. "In the name of your prince."

"Let 'our' prince see this," said yet another monster, stepping forward. This one had a scabby blue face, complete with a piggy snout. The horrible face was partially hidden beneath the hood of a brown cloak. But the creature's rage was palpable. While his not-so-jolly green compadre held Cedric in place, the blue guy raised his weapon. Its magic blade sparkled and crackled in the gloom of the maze.

Cornelia screamed. The monster was going to cut Cedric's head off! She couldn't watch.

But she also couldn't drag her horrified eyes away!

And she wasn't the only one!

Suddenly, Will burst from the cluster of Guardians.

"No!" she screamed.

She lunged between the rebel and Cedric, her hands outstretched. As she leapt to Cedric's aid, the Heart of Candracar erupted from her palm, shooting rays of bright-pink magic throughout the bookshop.

But the rebel had no time to react.

His sword came crashing down, slamming into the young Guardian.

"Will!" Cornelia shrieked. She felt Hay Lin clutch at her from behind while Taranee gasped in horror.

Then, an eerie, stunned silence filled the maze. Every Guardian and rebel was struck dumb by what they'd just seen.

For what they'd just seen was . . . unbelievable!

The sword had bounced off Will as if she had been made of rubber. There wasn't a scratch on her. Cedric, still crouching behind her, had not been injured.

As for Will's face, it was shocking as well. Instead of looking freaked or frightened in the wake of her near death, she was the picture of peace. In fact, she'd thrown her head back and thrust her hands out before her. She cradled the Heart of Candracar above her palms with grace and absolute authority.

Finally, one of the monsters broke the silence. His voice was thick with awe.

"It's a miracle," he breathed.

"Yes," agreed one of his comrades. "She's still alive!"

She was more than alive. She was levitating from the floor, buoyed by the great surges of magic pouring forth from the Heart of Candracar!

As she opened her mouth to speak, every ear strained to take in her wisdom.

It was then that Cornelia knew. Will was not just a leader. She was a hero. She'd risked her own life to save that of the Guardians' sworn enemy.

And if she was able to do that, Cornelia thought in wonder, I know she'll *never* fail her own friends. That's why I'll never let hurt feelings form a wedge between us again.

Only united, Cornelia thought determinedly, can W.i.t.c.h. save the world!

THEY MIGHT ACTUALLY SUCCEED IN CLOSING THE PORTAL.

I MUST STOP THEM. THE INVASION ONLY JUST STARTED!

WHERE ARE YOU GOING? THEY WILL SEE YOU AND . . .

LOOK, BROTHERS!

SHAZATZZZ

IT'S THE SERVANT OF PHOBOS! CATCH HIM!

HUH? WHAT ARE THEY DOING? ARE THEY AGAINST CEDRIC?

NOT AGAINST HIM, BUT AGAINST ALL THAT HE REPRESENTS!

"YEARS OF LIES! OF POVERTY!"

LET GO OF ME! IN THE NAME OF YOUR KING!

"OF SUFFERING!"

NOW, YOU'LL GET WHAT YOU DESERVE! IN THE NAME OF MERIDIAN!

GET OUT OF THE WAY, VATHEK! SHE AND HER FRIENDS WILL CLOSE THE PORTAL AGAIN!

KEEP HER AWAY! THIS IS THE ONLY WAY YOU'LL GAIN FREEDOM! A NEW WORLD WHERE . . .

IT'S USELESS. THEY WON'T DO IT!

THEY WILL COME BACK WITH ME TO THEIR . . . TO OUR WORLD!

DO I NEED TO REMIND YOU WHO'S IN CHARGE, YOU BIG BEAST? DO YOU KNOW WHO YOU ARE TALKING TO?

. . . AND I'VE DECIDED TO CHANGE IT! LET'S GO, BROTHERS!

TRAITOR! PHOBOS HIMSELF WILL MAKE YOU REGRET YOUR DECISION!

DO YOU WANT TO ELIMINATE THE ONLY PERSON WHO HAS STOOD BY YOU ALL YOUR MISERABLE LIFE?

WHAT'S GOING ON? WHAT'S HAPPENED TO YOU, VATHEK?

A LITTLE MIRACLE! I'VE SEEN TOO MUCH DARKNESS. . . .

I'LL WAIT FOR HIM WITH OPEN ARMS, IN THE DEPTHS OF MERIDIAN!

KWAAM

CEDRIC!

TAKE ME AWAY, ELYON! YOU ARE THE ONLY ONE I HAVE LEFT....

...ONLY YOU...

THAT WAS INCREDIBLE! FANTASTIC!

THOSE WORDS! HOW DID YOU KNOW WHAT TO SAY?

I—I DON'T KNOW! IT JUST CAME OUT OF MY MOUTH! AS IF I WAS SPEAKING FOR...

...SOMEONE ELSE...